E R

MAGI SALA

SELDOM, IF EVER, have I read a story so filled with love: passionate love, forbidden love, maternal love, love in all its wonderful, confusing, all-encompassing, at times tragic forms. And even in the face of heartbreak, a story about its enduring power.

This is a remarkable book, both prequel and sequel to Mulberry Dreams, filled with engaging characters who, as they search for meaning and happiness, find their lives intertwine in intriguing and, at times, shocking ways.

Maureen van der Horn

PRAISE FOR MULBERRY

THANK YOU for a marvellous read in 'Mulberry Dreams'. You paint marvellous pictures and the story has a singular narrative coherence. Well done and I look forward to your next novel! **J.W.**

I DEVOURED Mulberry Dreams like Calvin's first banana cake! I marvel at you being able to construct such a story which weaves so many levels of experience together; the social, the personal, the memories, the natural sensations, the sensuality, the language and colour, but above all, the drama and tension, driven by the arc of starting off not knowing oneself and learning, through a series of events, in which strangers are not strangers and differences are not differences...the veils are eventually drawn aside in a beautifully executed way, like the sweep of the Matador's red cape! Vague memories become crystal clear. What a good first book! **M.S.**

I FOUND the book compelling from start to finish, which is rare for me these days. The writing is spare but often beautiful and the story is moving. Please support Violette so that she writes another novel! **N.E.**

I HAVE at last indulged myself in a reading of Mulberry Dreams. I am exhausted yet exhilarated! Having threaded my way through intrigue, love, lust and longing, I never expected such an epic ending! My thoughts centre around guilt and contrition, I was one of those ancestral bigots whose parents slighted people of colour for many years. Thank goodness the era of enlightenment dawned and we refused to entertain our parents' intolerance. Your novel made me think more deeply, and I loved it! Beautifully written, quite unexpected, so many tiny topical gems to make one smile. I look forward to your next novel. **M.K.**

DREAMS

I ENJOYED reading Mulberry Dreams so much, from beginning to end. I couldn't put it down. It's superbly crafted. Congratulations, and I trust you will present us all with another before too long. ***J.T.***

I WAS reluctant to read Mulberry Dreams - my memories of that time and place being so bittersweet that I felt no-one could possibly articulate them. But you did, and then some. I cried, I laughed, I read the whole story from cover to cover in one sitting, not wanting it to end. I know those places, those people, that time. Thank you so very much for bringing them all back to life. ***A.P.***

I JUST finished reading this remarkable book. What a unique novel it is. As much as there is a lot of noise about Damon Galgut at present, I do think your writing as innovative and important. ***M.B.***

I FINISHED Mulberry Dreams in one day. I literally couldn't put it down. What an amazing story - I loved the way you kept us guessing right to the very end as to what happened - and of course a few good twists which I never would have come up with. A huge congratulations to you on this incredible achievement – I look forward to the next one. ***T.C.***

I STARTED reading Mulberry Dreams late this afternoon and have already finished it! It was absolutely enthralling and I found it very difficult to put down. You captured the essence of each character perfectly and for a time, I was in the world of Emma and Calvin. I grew up too living in mulberry bushes pretending to be in another world and it brought back many of my own precious childhood memories. ***M.T.***

Violette Kee-Tui

Magic and Masala

Pigeon Press

Published by Pigeon Press
12 Fortune's Gate Road, Bulawayo, Zimbabwe

For more information on this and other titles email:
info@hubbardstours.com

Cover Design: Daniel Mutendi
Cover Artist: Brian Mandizira
Text Design & Typesetting: Wayne Nel

ISBN 978-1-77921-178-1

To Emil and Katya,
who continue to believe in me despite my flaws,
and remain my greatest pride and inspiration.

To Paul, whose love is imprinted on me
as timelessly as his beloved rock art.

ACKNOWLEDGEMENTS

This is the part I love the most, but find the most difficult to write. Because how can I adequately express how much the support, the love, the encouragement, the technical assistance and belief in me from so many people has contributed to this book? It is beyond value and beyond words. However, I can not see *Magic and Masala* in print without it containing the names of those people in my life who made it possible – and continue to be in my corner no matter what. First on the list are my wonderful children, Emil and Katya, among my favourite people in the world. Their support and encouragement has kept me going so many times when I've wanted to give up. Katya had the misfortune of sharing a bedroom with me while we were visiting my darling parents in Florida in July 2022 - and the writing bug bit. I was up all hours, typing maniacally away at the laptop, fever dreaming plots and places and characters and waking her up to run scenarios past her which she so often helped me unpack, visualise and execute. My partner and best friend, Paul Hubbard, has once again been intrinsic in seeing *Magic and Masala* come to life. He is one of my most honest yet loving critics, and I appreciate all his input, from the gentle encouragement to the strictly business matter of publishing.

I'm proud, once again, to be publishing under his Pigeon Press label. John Eppel, that legend of a man and inspiration to all of us aspiring and published writers who hang on his every word, once again did a full edit for me, and his comments and corrections were, as always, transformative. Thanks also to Maureen van der Horn for doing a full reading with comments and feedback, as well as Charmaine Robinson whose eagle eye I can always trust. Thanks, also, to Hussein Rahman for checking and correcting the Arabic words and references to Islam. Wayne Nel has once again done an amazing job typesetting *Magic and Masala.* He makes the process seem effortless, even when it's not, and I will always value his patience and generosity. I'm also grateful to the very kind and accommodating Daniel Mutendi for designing the cover, using the magical original artwork of Bulawayo based artist, Brian Mandizira. I envisaged the cover in my mind, and Brian and Daniel made it a reality. A couple of people suggested a family tree would be a good addition to the book and I'd like to say a big thank you to Tammy Honiball for doing such a wonderful one for the book. A huge thank you, also, to my dear friends, Nyasha and Norman Monks, who helped make the printing possible and whose generosity and kindness never fails to astonish me. My beautiful parents and my siblings and their families, together with Paul's wonderful family, have once again been an important part of this journey, as have so many friends and supporters around the world who were so generous in their feedback about *Mulberry Dreams* and encouraged me to keep writing. *Mulberry Dreams* was going to be a one-and-done. I truly didn't see a second novel in my future. But as is the way with the creative process, a story started brewing inside me. A new character, Sharifa, began to form out of mid air and I very soon found myself half in love with this beautiful, imaginary woman. Sharifa still lives with me, inside me, long after I have finished writing *Magic and Masala* and I look for her all the time, everywhere I go. She's made up of parts of all the women I've admired and loved and rooted for, all the women I've aspired to be. Above all, she's the love that refuses to give up.

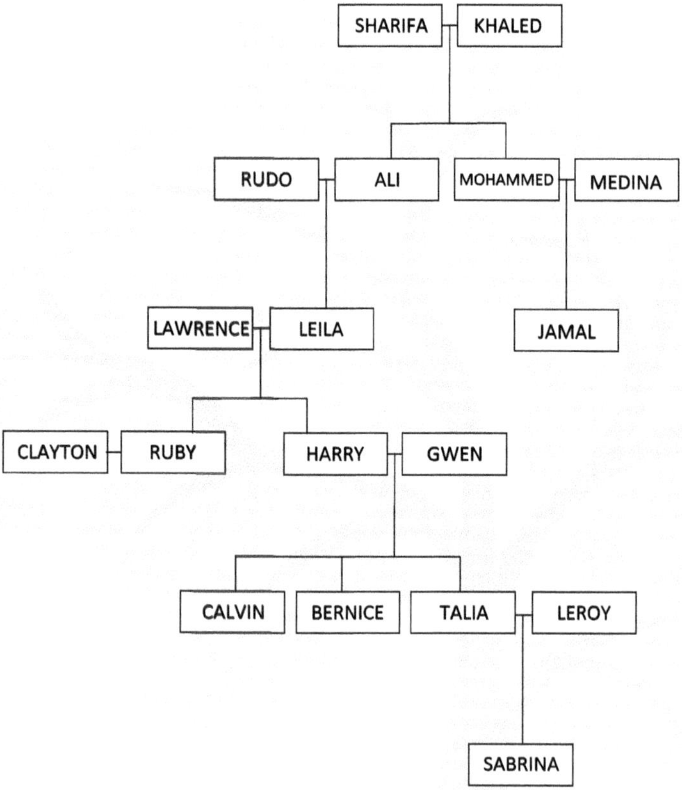
SHARIFA
KHALED
RUDO
ALI
MOHAMMED
MEDINA
LAWRENCE
LEILA
JAMAL
CLAYTON
RUBY
HARRY
GWEN
CALVIN
BERNICE
TALIA
LEROY
SABRINA

PROLOGUE

1953

NANI SHARIFA BROUGHT magic and masala when she came to visit that summer. She also brought a secret. The magic was in a deep, dark box that smelt of woodsmoke and, if they were very good, Nani would let Harry and Ruby look inside. Resting in the velvety darkness were different sized crystals which glistened and glowed when she lifted the lid and let in the light. This one is for tranquility, she would tell the children, holding up a bright white moonstone; this one is for protection, she'd say showing them a small green aquamarine, the colour of the sea. And this one, this one is very, very special, she would whisper, cradling a pink quartz in her wrinkled brown palm and holding it up to the light. This one is for love. And her eyes would fill with shadows.

The masala was for her cooking and, oh boy, could Nani cook! The smells would make the children's tummies rumble and even though it was sometimes so spicy it made their eyes water, they'd finish every morsel all the same.

And her secret? Nani Sharifa had carried the secret with her so long it had become a part of her, worn into the lines of her face, its burden carved into the round of her back. When Nani Sharifa travelled all the way from Cape Town to Bulawayo that summer, she was finally ready to lay it down.

CHAPTER ONE

2015

THE NEIGHBOURS SET their watches to Harry's morning walk around the block; come rain or shine, they see the old man's small, grey crocheted beanie bob just above their walls, and they know it's 6 o'clock.

These days Harry finds himself lingering more and more in the past. His little sister, Ruby, playing beside him in the dusty paths near their home – Ruby, with two broccoli-shaped bunches of hair attached to either side of her head, the short strands pulled so tight she'd cry every morning as Mama tried to tie them up. Her hair so different to Mama's long, straight tresses. Ruby, in her favourite pink dress, high-waisted with two lengths that started off prettily tied at the back in a belt and, within minutes, were fluttering behind her as she ran – like the brightly-coloured ribbons on a Maypole.

And Harry himself, never without a stick in his hand – for poking, for digging, for defending, for playing soldier boy or farmer or dinosaur hunter. (Much like now, he thinks, glancing down at his walking stick and smiling). His shortie shorts with snaps to close them at the waist – usually unsnapped for comfort – his once-white shirt, grubby and grey by lunchtime, trailing half open where the buttons had popped.

Their mother would look despairingly when she called them in at the end of each day.

"Harry Donovan Rhoades! Just look at you! And your little sister! You'll be the death of me!"

Before dinner, they'd help their mother fill buckets of water from the well at the end of the plot, each taking a side of the rim though, to be honest, Ruby was just there for show. Harry would walk on tiptoes, doing his best to lift the bucket up to his chest to be level with his mother and try not to spill. But he inevitably became distracted or bored or tired and the precious liquid would swish and splash onto their feet.

"Harry!" his mother would shout. "Just leave it!"

And he'd watch, momentarily mortified, to see his mother kick off her shoes so she wouldn't slip on the mud his carelessness had created, and struggle to carry the bucket alone; but he'd soon become distracted by a butterfly or a passing bicycle bell, or the sound of dogs barking on the street, and forget all about her.

Mother would gather logs from a pile that sat outside the kitchen door and fire up the wood stove to heat the water, the small, bright kitchen turning instantly dark with smoke. By the time the water was warm, the smoke would have lifted and she'd fill a galvanised tub in the kitchen with one part hot and two parts cold, and they'd both jump in, the afternoon sun streaming in through the windows and bathing them in light. Their bodies would displace the water a little, so at least it covered their knees, and they'd be instructed to scrub their feet and their underarms and between their legs, "all the hot spots", mother would say. The lime left the water thick with scum, so mother would always keep one bucket of warm water aside to rinse them off. The water always cooled down too fast, no matter the weather, and they would stand up and brace themselves when mother poured that last bucket over them.

Then it was into their pyjamas and time for dinner. Ruby got Harry's hand-me-downs, usually blue and sometimes festooned with aeroplanes. Harry wore his till they were several inches above his ankles, so that in winter his feet were always ice cold.

Their father rarely made it home for dinner. Leila learnt a long time ago not to question her husband or he'd stay out later. Harry didn't have any memories of his parents fighting. He didn't have any memories of them as his parents.

These are the thoughts Harry carries with him, all these years later, as he walks.

It had been almost five years since Calvin had inherited the small house at number 17 from Mrs. Calderwood and moved Harry in with him. Calvin's youngest sister, Talia, and her daughter, Sabrina, had moved in a few months earlier and the siblings had together decided to look after their father.

Sabrina, 15 years old at the time, became Harry's solace. They were kindred spirits from the start, both trapped in silence for different reasons, and would sit together for hours, he in his wheelchair, she propped up with cushions on the sofa, neither saying a word but comforted by each other's presence.

Harry eventually thawed, found his voice – very slowly and very quietly. But Sabrina never would. And now that he was on the other side, Harry became her caregiver. His granddaughter's dark eyes lit up every time Harry walked into the room and the only sound she ever made – a sound so close to joy it made everyone around them smile – was when he was near.

Sabrina helped him heal, and Harry wished he could return the favour.

"Come on, my girl, just one more bite," he'd coax at meal times, sitting opposite her on the couch and spoon feeding her. "How will you ever grow big and strong if you don't eat? Now, did I ever tell you the story about when Granny Ruby and I tried to steal oranges from the priest's house and got chased by his billy goat?" And he'd chuckle a deep, throaty chuckle, and although Sabrina couldn't understand a word, she'd gurgle happily.

Talia had found a job at a local supermarket where she worked long hours and came home every night exhausted. Calvin was either working or "off with who knows who this time", Harry would mutter to Sabrina, so it was a relief to everyone that the pair had each other.

Once Harry had forced himself to learn to walk again, at first haltingly up and down the driveway, then up the street and back and, finally, right around the block, he no longer needed the wheelchair and began lifting Sabrina into it, pushing her gently up and down the driveway each afternoon before dinner. Those were the times he loved the best:

the viscous twilight coating everything in lucid light, the last of the bird song for the day, the breeze after the heat of the day…and Sabrina. He would tell her their family stories as they walked and Sabrina would gurgle.

Harry convinced Calvin to buy some hens and it became his job to tend them, walking to the back behind the mulberry tree to scatter chicken feed and table scraps each morning and, as they grew, collect their eggs. Thanks to Harry, there were always fresh eggs with bright yellow yolks for breakfast.

It was impossible for Harry to walk to the back of the garden and not think of Margot – a sweet anguish he couldn't resist. The little room he'd used on the nights he'd stayed on the property all those years ago during the war had hardly changed: still the same dark walls, the same gloomy interior, illuminated, in his imagination, by the light of Margot's presence.

He wouldn't allow himself the luxury or the pain of thinking too long about her, or allowing his thoughts to wander back to that day. But sometimes, no matter how hard he tried, he couldn't keep the thoughts at bay – and almost always, on those days, he'd retreat into his silence and forget how to walk again. Then he'd remember Sabrina and rouse himself to prepare her lunch. And he'd be brought back to life by the light in his granddaughter's eyes when he walked into the room.

Some days as he walked, Harry's thoughts wandered further back still – to a time and a place he knew only through the stories his mother would tell them, once they were tucked up in bed and ready to sleep. His favourite memories of her. Once she'd finished their bed-time story, she'd kiss them each on the crowns of their heads and remind them not to open the door to anyone, then she'd lock the front door and they'd hear the creak of the front gate as she swung it shut, before starting her long walk to work. Leila worked night shift at a popular ice cream parlour and wouldn't finish till way after 10 o'clock. By the time she walked home it would be close to midnight, and the children were always too fast asleep to hear her come in. Some mornings Harry would wake up in a panic, worrying that he hadn't heard her and maybe she hadn't come home. He'd race through to the kitchen but she'd always be there, already busy with the morning's chores.

Harry loved to hear the stories of how his grandparents had met and now, in adulthood and after all that had happened, he realised how much of his grandfather lived in him; more than his green eyes, he shared with Ali an immeasurable capacity for love and passion – at any cost.

CHAPTER TWO

Cape Town 1919

FOR A LONG time after they boarded the ship and as it laboured away from the shore, Mohammed would stand at the railing, gripping the cold steel and watching the gradually diminishing figure of his father, arm raised in farewell – until it became a tiny speck on the smudge of horizon and then disappeared altogether, swallowed by the expanse of sea between them. They'd said goodbye to their mother at the house – the docks are no place for a woman, Sharifa! – his father had snapped, dismissing her with a flick of his hand when she'd begged to see them off. Mohammed had wrapped his arms around her as tight as he could, hoping to absorb her shuddering sobs and carry the burden of sadness for her. He could still smell her scarf pressed under his chin as he'd held her – the familiar sweet and spicy of jasmine and masala – and still see her small, veiled form through the tiny window, barely illuminated by the early dawn light.

He finally let go of the railing and went in search of Ali, and wasn't surprised when he found his younger brother below deck at the centre of a large group of laughing men.

Ali went up on his tip toes and started shouting excitedly when he saw him, his green eyes shining. "Mohammed! Mohammed! Come meet my new friends! Everyone, this is Mohammed, my big brother!" And he was immediately welcomed into the circle.

"Any brother of Ali, is a brother of ours!" said a large, bald man, a massive hand on Ali's shoulder. And Mohammed tried his best to smile.

The boys were bound for Southern Rhodesia where their father's cousin had opened a fabric shop in the fledgling town of Bulawayo and offered them a job and a place to stay – and with no prospects of work in the Cape, it was an opportunity they couldn't pass up.

They travelled steerage and in the dark, damp, crowded quarters not even Ali's sense of humour and ability to make friends could make it any more tolerable. Their ship ran into stormy waters on the second day at sea and they finally arrived in Beira two long weeks later – emaciated by sea sickness and poor nutrition – and started to make their way to Bulawayo.

It was an arduous 21-day journey by road, rail, horse cart and, at one point, driven by desperation to reach the safety of the border settlement of Umtali before dark, donkey.

When the boys finally arrived in the dusty settlement of Bulawayo, they were filthy, exhausted and homesick for the ocean.

Uncle Mustafa, as he urged them to call him, was welcoming and warm, a round-bellied man who laughed often and loudly and who wasted no time introducing the boys to their new routine, waking them that first morning before dawn for prayers.

The shop was in one of four long roads designated for Blacks: cramped, dimly-lit stores with tin rooves, squeezed shoulder to shoulder at the end of town and run mostly by Indians, newly-arrived from India, Pakistan and South Africa.

It was dank and grey and, when they saw it for the first time – early on a winter morning – depressing. Uncle Mustafa lit a paraffin lamp to offer some illumination until, finally, the watery light began to filter in through the small, high windows, and he set the boys to work.

The fabric arrived by ship in the port city of Lourenco Marques then travelled by rail to Bulawayo, the huge rolls so heavy it took two people to lift them. The boys' first task was to roll them out and measure them. It took hours to do one roll, a tedious job in the half-light with a tiny measuring tape.

The boys measured hundreds of metres of fabric that first week: bright, Indian cotton and richly-jewelled satins, colourful ethnic prints from Java – a favourite of the locals, worn tied at the waist like a skirt – heavy-duty drill and vividly-coloured cotton prints.

Mohammed recorded the measurements on long scrolls of manila paper, sketched in his small, precise hand, and at the end of each day, their backs aching from all the lifting, they handed them to Uncle Mustafa. The boys were quick and efficient and never complained, at least not openly. But at night as they lay side by side on thin, straw mattresses on the concrete floor of Uncle Mustafa's spare room, Ali would start grumbling quietly to his older brother.

"I'm tired and my back hurts."

"Quiet, Ali," said Mohammed, "they'll hear you."

"I don't care if they hear me, what kind of job is this? I thought we were done with being slaves! I want to go home."

"Be quiet and go to sleep. We're here now, we have no choice. Get some rest and give me some peace."

Ali carried on muttering softly to himself until he finally fell asleep.

Later they would learn that Uncle Mustafa had given them the task to see what they were made of.

"They're good boys," he told Mr. Jina who ran the discount grocery store next door. "Honest, hard-working boys, a credit to their parents. I think it's time we found them wives." He stroked his bearded chin.

"Who did you have in mind?" asked Jina, squinting up at him through thick, round spectacles.

"How about old man Ahmed's daughters? Fine young women, both of them."

"They're old enough to be the boys' mothers – and one of them has a beard!" snorted Jina.

"The boys would be lucky to have them, decent young women, Nur I Islam – the light of Islam!"

Jina shrugged.

The boys were promoted a month after they arrived, making the transition from stock room to the front of shop – and when Uncle Mustafa gave them the news he beamed with pride.

"Anyone would think we'd won a motor car," grumbled Ali that evening.

Although he was completely satisfied with their work, Uncle Mustafa still wasn't sure if they were ready to serve customers.

"No talking to the customers, no giving advice or commenting on fabrics – you're not yet experienced enough," said Uncle Mustafa, wagging a fat finger in the air in time to his shaking head. "Just wait for instructions to measure out the rolls. But don't despair my boys, the way you're going it won't be long before you're promoted to sales assistants!" he said, slapping Mohammed on the back.

"Yippee," said Ali under his breath, and Mohammed jabbed him swiftly in the ribs.

Soon the boys had fitted so well into the routine of the household it was as if they'd been there all their lives.

Each day before dawn Uncle Mustafa would wake them for Fajr which they would do in the back room, kneeling towards Ka'bah and chanting quietly under their breaths in the sweet guttural tones of Arabic. After prayers his wife, Auntie Nasreen, would feed them a hearty breakfast of rice and brisket curry so tender the meat would be falling off the bone, and they would head for the shop.

The shop was one block away from the house and they would make the short walk mostly in silence, Mohammed because he was still quietly meditating on the sacred words of the Koran, Ali because he was still half asleep.

Uncle Mustafa would arrive at the shop at exactly 7 o'clock, and his staff would be waiting at the door. He was a strict but fair employer who insisted on punctuality.

They would spend an hour sweeping and organising the shop for its opening at 8 o'clock.

There were only two breaks during the day, both marked by prayer time. At midday Auntie Nasreen would deliver their lunch and Uncle Mustafa would wash his hands over a blue plastic tub at the back of the shop, quickly perform his Dhuhr prayers, and eat while standing at the till, raised on a platform so he had a full view of the shop floor at all times.

Mohammed and Ali were allowed 15 minutes to go to the back and do the same. Lunch was delivered in tiffin boxes and usually consisted of chicken curry, rich with masala and a sharp bite of chilli, spicy potatoes and rotis. The boys would eat in the traditional way, holding the plate close to their chins with their left hand and deftly scooping the food into their mouths with their right.

As soon as they were done, they would wash their hands again, their fingers still smudged yellow with spices, hand the containers to Auntie Nasreen to take back to the house, and carry on with their work. The second break was mid-afternoon, to perform Asr, and the boys would take the opportunity afterwards to walk outside for a few minutes of fresh air, blinking in the harsh sunlight after the gloom of the storeroom

The shop closed at 5 o'clock on the dot. Then another half hour would be spent cashing up before Uncle Mustafa threaded the thick chain through the handle on the front door and fastened it with a huge steel lock.

"Can never be too careful," he'd say, "these people love to steal."

Then they'd walk back to the house in time for Maghrib, dinner and bed.

Besides the short walk to the shop and Mr. Jina's store next door, the boys never saw Auntie Nasreen leave the house. She would be there every day when they returned, her head scarf pulled tight around her face to cover every last strand of her hair, her hands constantly moving over the fire, stirring, tasting, adding seasoning, half-hidden like a genie in the swirls of steam rising from the massive pots.

At dinner time she would silently lay the food on the table and return to the kitchen, leaving the men to their meal. Once they had had their fill and left the table, she would sit down and eat, and then clear the table and wash the dishes.

Ali wondered what time she had to wake up to have breakfast ready for them by 6 o'clock – always freshly made, never leftovers. It made him think of his mother, how she would be on her feet from before they woke up and long after she tucked them into bed. If he'd woken in the night, no matter the time, he would hear her padding softly around the small house, washing dishes and putting them away, folding the laundry and making preparations for the next day's meals. And he'd feel his chest tighten, unable to separate the comfort he'd felt hearing the gentle sounds of her moving around the house with the guilt he felt now for never appreciating all she did.

The weekends were the boys' only time for a little rest and recreation. On Saturday afternoons, once the shop had closed, they'd be allowed to spend time with some of the other young men in the community, with Ali more often than not in the centre of a heated game of cards by the end of the day. On Sundays, Uncle Mustafa would make a special point to sit with the boys and further their Islamic instruction. Ali always marvelled at how rapt Mohammed would sit and listen, leaning forward and absorbing every single word, while he fidgeted in his seat, his mind wandering, counting the minutes until it would be over.

And so the boys' routine continued, day in and day out, with little variation.

Mohammed, if he was unhappy, never complained. Ali never stopped. He missed everything about home: the sea, his friends, his mother, even, sometimes, his father's constant remonstrations.

"I want to go home, Mohammed," he'd tell his brother. "I hate it here."

Mohammed would tell him to stop being such a child.

"This is home now, Ali."

Eventually the boys moved up to the position of sales assistant and, within a year, the ultimate promotion: handling the till. So great had Uncle Mustafa's trust and admiration of the boys grown that there were even one or two occasions – albeit for only 10 or 15 minutes at a time – when he would leave them in charge of the entire shop while he went next door to visit Jina.

He was now working in earnest to find the boys wives. He'd passed the word around the community that they were ready to marry, promoting the fact that they were good boys from an upstanding Moslem family.

"They are doing very well in the business; they're hard workers and would provide well for their families," he told a gathering of men after evening prayers at the small, squat building in the Black township that served as the community's first Mosque. "Since Allah has not blessed me with children of my own, they are like my own sons and will take over the business when I'm old."

Of course everyone knew Uncle Mustafa would carry on working in the shop until the day he died, most probably taking his last breath while counting up the money for a metre of cotton drill, they would chuckle amongst themselves. But still it was a fine tribute to the high esteem in which Mohammed and Ali were held by their uncle.

Finally, word came that two suitable young women had

been found. They were from Salisbury and seemed to come with good credentials. Uncle Mustafa was delighted. He could hardly wait to tell the boys when he gathered them together at dinner time.

"Boys," and his double chin wobbled with delight, "I have good news, wonderful news in fact!"

"Good news? What is it, Uncle?" replied Mohammed excitedly. Ali raised one eyebrow and waited.

"I have found you wives!" And he threw his arms in the air.

"You've found us what!" Now it was Ali who spoke.

Mohammed laid a hand on his arm.

"Uncle, you've found us wives?" There was a mixture of surprise and pleasure on Mohammed's beatific face.

"Yes, that's right!" he said, ignoring Ali's incredulous stare and focussing on Mohammed's wide-eyed pleasure, his dark eyes bright.

"Who are they?" asked Ali.

"Ali, all we need to know is that Uncle has looked into the family and he approves." Mohammed's tone was cautionary.

"When will we meet them?" asked Ali.

"There'll be no time for meeting them! What for?" said Uncle Mustafa, spreading his arms wide. "We have a wedding to arrange!"

"I refuse!" said Ali the minute he and Mohammed were alone in their room.

"You refuse? You refuse! You have no right to accept or refuse; this is your destiny."

"This is not destiny, this is business!"

"This isn't your decision to make, Ali! Uncle Mustafa has

our best interests at heart, as would our parents if they were here. We're of the age to be married and we should be grateful that we've been saved the trouble of finding someone suitable ourselves. When do you imagine we would have found time to do that? Where would we have even started looking?"

"You expect me to marry a stranger, someone I've never met?"

"You won't be the first or the last, Ali. Grow up!"

Ali railed against the idea every night once they retreated to their rooms. Mohammed would always tell him the same thing: that he had no say in the matter. The wedding was to go ahead.

There was great excitement in the household from the day of Uncle Mustafa's announcement, and Auntie Nasreen would spend hours planning with the other women from the community, organising meals, arranging what to wear. It was a small community and weddings were still a rarity.

The Mendi was planned for April 6th, exactly one month to the day of Uncle Mustafa's announcement.

It would be held at the Mosque, once they closed the shop, and as the boys' father would not be able to attend, Uncle Mustafa would stand in for him.

The two boys approached the event as differently as they approached most things in life: Mohammed with pious reflection and prayer, Ali with barely contained resentment.

Mohammed knew his brother better than anyone on earth; he knew his weaknesses, knew his kindly heart and strong will. Mohammed thought he'd seen it all when it came to Ali, that nothing he could do would ever surprise him.

But one week before the wedding Ali did something which shocked even his brother.

He ran away.

CHAPTER THREE

2015

CALVIN WAS DOING refurbishment work for a family who'd recently lost their father. He'd been a renowned local artist and Calvin came home one day with a box full of things the family was throwing out.

"I thought you'd smaak these." Calvin planted a cardboard box on the table in front of Harry before walking back out the door.

Harry smelt the sharp sting of acetone on the dried brushes before he saw what was inside, and a hundred sensations raced through him.

A heart-shaped face, hair the colour of honey, head thrown back and laughing. The garden behind her a beautiful riot of life and colour, all pale in comparison to her. His mind went back to that day, sitting on the steps painting Margot's portrait, her children, Emma and Peter, sitting on either side of him as he worked. Running off to play and then scooting back to check on his progress. Peter knew exactly who it was and when he told little Emma, she laughed with delight and clapped her hands.

He'd taken the portrait to his room and that night when Margot had come to the back to meet him, as she did every night when her husband, David, was on call-up duty, it was standing on the window sill to dry. She'd taken it in her hands and stood looking at it for the longest time. His heart was pounding. When, finally, she turned back to look at him, still holding it in her hands, her eyes were bright with tears.

"You make me look so beautiful," she'd said quietly.

"You're the most beautiful woman I've ever seen." And his voice broke as he said it.

She'd set it back on the window sill and walked over to where he was sitting on the edge of the bed, then she'd sat beside him and laid her head on his shoulder. He'd taken her hand and interlaced his fingers with hers, and they'd sat like that for the longest time, neither trusting themselves to speak.

"Come, my girl, squeeze your fingers together, hold it."

Harry was holding a paintbrush between Sabrina's fingers with one hand and pressing her fingers down around it with the other.

"Squeeze, my girl, squeeze. You can do it."

Harry could see the light shift in her eyes.

He pressed down and let go and the paintbrush fell on the ground. He picked it up and tried again. And again. Until, finally, after 10 or more attempts, the paintbrush stayed between her fingers when he let go – just for a moment before clattering back down to the floor.

"You did it, my girl, you did it!" Detecting the tone in his voice, Sabrina gurgled.

They tried again the next day. And the next. And by the end of the week Sabrina was holding the brush for several minutes at a time, tightening her grip around it a little more each day.

By the second week Harry had her propped up under the shade of the syringa tree in the front yard, a plastic apron around her neck, a piece of paper on a kitchen tray in front of her and a paintbrush in her hand.

"Now, my girl, we paint!"

He sat beside her, placed the paintbrush in her hand and guided it into a saucer of water, then, the tip wet, into a pallet of children's watercolours and onto the paper. The pair made rainbow swirls all afternoon, bright arches of happy colour filling the page and splattering around them, Harry gently coaxing her.

By the end of the day Harry realised she would never be able to do it alone, but it became their little afternoon ritual, sitting under the shade of the tree or, on cold and windy days, on the veranda, painting rainbows together.

Initially Harry didn't dare touch the oils himself, or take up his own paintbrush. But he kept the box on his dresser and every time he'd pass, he'd catch a scent of the acetone and feel his heart quicken all over again.

After Harry moved in, Clayton, Ruby's husband and Harry's oldest friend, would regularly stop by to visit. In the early days before Harry was talking, the two would sit side-by-side in the sun, Clayton carrying on a one-way conversation, talking to him about the things they'd done as boys and all the people they'd known over the years.

One day, about a month in, Clayton was regaling Harry with a story of one of their childhood pranks.

"There you were, caught red-handed by that sour old Mrs. Tucker, the whoopee cushion in your hands!" And Clayton threw back his head and roared with laughter.

"It was yours."

It was said so softly, Clayton almost missed it. He swung around to look at his friend.

"What? What did you say?"

"I said it was yours," said Harry, still softly – no more than a whisper – but much more confidently this time and with the tiniest smile out of the corner of his mouth.

"You old rascal, you've been harbouring that one all these years, haven't you?" chuckled Clayton, and pushed his old friend gently on his arm.

Their conversations slowly developed from there, Harry still the quieter of the two, as he always had been.

Clayton caught Harry up on all the news – who was doing what, who was sleeping with who, who had died and who'd just become a grandparent.

"You remember old Mr. Greenland from the Terraces?"

"With the club foot?" asked Harry.

"Yup, that's the one. Remember he had a son, Lionel, a nasty piece of work?" said Clayton, sitting on the low wall, his hands on his bony knees and shaking his head. "Always getting into trouble with the law. Knocked up old Chookie Pieters' daughter, a pretty young thing she was, doing so well at school too, and then runs away to South Africa.

"Anyway, he gets involved in who knows what that side and makes bundles of money. Comes back here driving the latest Mercedes, throwing cash all over the place. Doesn't so much as drop in to see his new born child. Some boys from the neighbourhood, they decide to teach him a lesson – one of them was Pieters' son, I think, sore as hell for how Lionel had treated his little sister.

"They find out he's messing around with old Terrence McKop's wife – yes, the same Terrence who left school to become a boxer – and they tip Terrence off when Lionel is visiting his missus.

"Well, wasn't it a sight – or so I'm told – Terrence storming in, full of violent fury, and Lionel, butt naked except for the gold chain around his neck, running out the back door to his Merc.

"But that's not the end of it! The boys had let the air out of his tyres and Lionel was caught, with his pants down, so to speak! Got the hiding of his life – couldn't have happened to a better person!" said Clayton, chuckling and slapping his knees.

The two old friends would laugh and talk for hours, skirting, for the time being anyway, any serious topics.

CHAPTER FOUR

1922

ON REFLECTION, MOHAMMED thought he should have seen it coming; but the truth was, nothing and no-one could have stopped Ali. When his parents had forced him to leave the Cape and come to Rhodesia he had protested, but no-one listened. When he was forced to work in the fabric shop for Uncle Mustafa, he had protested but, again, no-one listened.

Now he had protested having the rest of his life decided for him, and still no-one listened. He was damned if he was going to be sentenced to a life-time bondage in which he had no say.

No-one had quite anticipated the shame and loss of face Uncle Mustafa would experience, not even Ali himself. If he had, Mohammed sometimes wondered, would he have stayed?

The double wedding was called off, the fine clothes put away, the food discarded. There was outrage from the families of the brides and even the business took a knock, members of the community shunning Uncle Mustafa and Auntie Nasreen and whispering behind their backs that Ali had been possessed by a jinn.

Even though he had nothing to do with it, Mohammed shared the shame and the guilt.

Eventually, through some nifty negotiation on Uncle Mustafa's part and holding together the last shreds of his shattered reputation, he managed to convince the one family – eager to get their daughter married off – to marry Mohammed, and a small, simple Nikkah was held one quiet morning at the Mosque.

Mohammed prayed hard to Allah to forgive Ali for what he had done; he was grateful that He had still made the way clear for him to marry and had faith that He would in time bring his errant young brother back into the fold.

He and his new bride moved into a tiny apartment above Jina's shop and he resolved not to let Ali's actions tarnish his happiness.

Meanwhile Ali, always resourceful, made his way to Salisbury where there were more opportunities and fewer of Uncle Mustafa's connections.

He found a job with a Hindu family as a sales assistant in their fruit and vegetable store, and rented a room not much larger than a cupboard at the back of the local auction house around the corner.

And that was when he met Rudo.

Rudo was 14 years old when her parents pulled her out of school and sent her out to work, her father reasoning that the money would be far better spent on her younger brother.

She was employed as a cleaner in the vegetable shop, in charge of sweeping out the cabbage and lettuce leaves, fallen on the floor and trampled underfoot by customers, throwing out the rotting tomatoes and potatoes, piled high in a sweating fly-infested heap at the back, and keeping the shelves dusted and clean.

By the time Ali started working for the Patels she was going on 16, her boyish straight hips just starting to swell into curves. She had skin the colour of roasted coffee beans and Ali imagined it smelt like them too.

She acted like he didn't exist, and Ali was utterly captivated. He found himself dreaming about her, waking up sweating and frustrated, with no idea what to do.

This was treacherous ground even for Ali. A Black woman. But then his standing with his family couldn't really get much worse, he convinced himself. And, besides, he was never going back.

Ali finally found an opportunity to talk to her one blistering Saturday in October. It had been busy in the shop and the waste was immense and putrid. Rudo was battling with crates of spoilt bananas which she'd been instructed to carry out to the alleyway. The fruit flies buzzed around her face and flew into her eyes, making it even harder for her to carry the heavy crates.

Taking his chance when the stream of customers thinned, Ali went over to her and started to help.

"What are you doing?" she asked.

"Helping you."

"Why?"

"Because you look like you need it."

She didn't reply, but allowed him to take one of the heavier crates. He helped her with the rest, neither saying another word.

When they'd finished, she nodded slightly in his direction and walked away.

He watched her with his usual sense of longing and loss.

Although the shop closed at lunchtime on Saturdays, the day had been so busy that it was way after closing time when Mr. Patel locked the shop and they were all allowed to go home.

Ali had been so busy he hadn't seen Rudo again. When everyone else left, he walked around to the back of the shop through the dingy alleyway.

There she was, washing her hands and face in a tub of water before slipping behind the post to change from her work clothes into a clean dress. Ali caught sight of a smooth bare shoulder and quickly turned away.

He walked back to the mouth of the alleyway and waited. She carried a plastic bag containing her dirty work clothes and had tied a fresh scarf over her soft curls.

She rounded the corner and there he was. She didn't seem surprised to see him, and there was the faintest shadow of a smile on her full lips.

There was so much he wanted to say but he couldn't find the words. She smiled a tiny bit more now, the one corner of her mouth pulling slightly upwards and, in that one gesture, Ali found the courage to speak.

"Would you like to go for a drink?"

Their first date was outside a general dealers, sitting on a low wall with their feet dangling above the pavement and sipping icy cold lemonade, milky white with frost, through striped yellow straws.

Afterwards they walked down the street, full of late afternoon shoppers heading home before dark. Ali brushed the back of his hand against hers and then, tentatively, reached for her soft, cool fingers. When she didn't pull her hand away, he held on tightly and they kept on walking.

Ali was a free agent now, an outcast, but Rudo still had family and community constraints, so their meetings had to be held in secret, always furtive and rushed, always looking over their shoulders to make sure no-one was watching.

But over days and, then, weeks, they grew bolder.

One Saturday after work Rudo told her parents she was working late in the shop and, instead, went with Ali to his tiny room at the back of the auction house.

Ali held her hand in his and closed the door – and he would always remember her slow, shy, lopsided smile before the darkness shut them in.

Rudo's parents were beginning to suspect there was something going on. They'd started to notice a certain awakening in their daughter. She no longer walked with her eyes to the ground but stood up tall and looked straight ahead.

She took extra care with her appearance and was always working late at the shop.

The day her cousin, Tafadzwa, was assigned by Rudo's father to follow her and see what she was up to, was also the first day she realised something wasn't quite right.

Tafadzwa stood in the shadows of an adjoining shop and saw Rudo retreat down the alleyway once Mr. Patel had closed up and walked away. The shop emptied, except for a skinny Indian boy with striking green eyes who held back till everyone had left; then, glancing behind him, he followed Rudo down the alleyway.

Tafadzwa gave them a few minutes before heading down the dirty corridor. He rounded the corner and there they were, their arms around each other, the Indian's hands low on Rudo's back.

It seemed to happen in slow motion and, for Rudo, it took a moment for her to register that the savage animal howl was coming from her cousin, plummeting towards them, a look of raw rage on his face. Before either of them could react, Tafadzwa shoved Rudo out of the way and flung himself on Ali, throwing him to the ground and punching him over and over again in the face. Ali tried to defend himself but was no match for Tafadzwa's strength and anger.

Both men were so caught up in the moment neither noticed Rudo bent over double and vomiting into the dust.

CHAPTER FIVE

2015

SUNDAY WAS THE one day the family would all be at home together. Sometimes Bernice would stop in with her two boys, and about once a month Clayton and Ruby would call ahead and tell them they were bringing over Sunday lunch.

Ruby's Sunday lunches were legendary, an eclectic collection of recipes gathered from both branches of the family tree and always including at least one curry, rich with her own glorious pot-pourri of whole spices, roasted and ground together in a wooden pestle-and-mortar to make her garam masala. The pestle-and-mortar, handed down to her by her mother, carried the aroma of generations of cardamon and cinnamon, coriander and cumin deep in its grain and, as a child, Harry loved to smell it, reaching up on his tip toes to lift the mortar off the kitchen counter, holding it with both hands and bringing it up to his face so he could take a good, long sniff.

Ruby would serve her curry with rotis, flattened and rolled into seemingly perfect circles with a long, thin, handle-less rolling pin given to her by her Gogo Rudo, and fried lightly on each side on an upturned cast iron frying pan. Her famous macaroni and cheese was a favourite of her father's, or so her mother used to tell her, and no one could guess what the secret ingredient was which made it so rich and creamy – though if you'd asked Ruby, she'd smile and wink and tell you "love". If Clayton had managed to get to the butchery on Fridays when they offered a 10 percent discount to pensioners, there would be a brisket roast – and somehow, in Ruby's magical hands, this quite ordinary, budget cut of meat would be succulent and tender as a sirloin, the roast potatoes which accompanied them always the perfect combination of crisp skins and fluffy centres.

When they came over one Sunday late in May, the perfect azure skies already starting to peel back white in the late-afternoons as winter started to drift in, Ruby added a creamy cauliflower soup to her menu. To keep out the chills, she'd said, smiling her dimpled smile.

"Howzit, Uncle Clay, Auntie Rube," Calvin bent down to hug Ruby before shaking hands with Clayton, then walked over to the stove, lifted the lid to one of the huge steel pots and inhaled deeply. "Shit, that smells amazing, Auntie Rube! Don't ya just wanna move in with us? I scheme I've eaten enough of Talia's egg on toast to last me a lifetime!"

Talia leaned over and slapped him on the arm, "If you don't like it, maybe you can try cooking for a change!"

After lunch and before Ruby served afternoon tea and a slice of her famous double-layered chocolate cake, Clayton and Harry went outside to sit on the veranda.

They sat for a long time, full from the lunch and comfortable in each other's silence.

Then, in a voice so low Clayton almost didn't hear him, Harry asked: "Where's she buried?"

"What?" Clayton swung around to look at him.

"Where is she buried?" he repeated.

Clayton let out a long sigh. "The Greenwich Cemetery, in the section reserved for Whites in the old days."

"Will you take me there?"

"This, still, Harry? After all this time?" Clayton closed his eyes and shook his head from side to side.

"Time hasn't changed anything. And I never said goodbye." His voice was unsteady.

"You know I'd do anything for you, my old friend, but I don't see what good could come of this."

"Clayton, I need this. I have so little left. Of her."

"And what do you think it will solve?"

"Nothing. It won't solve anything. But I need this," he repeated.

Clayton was quiet for a long time.

A few days later Harry was sitting under the syringa tree painting with Sabrina when he heard a car pull up at the gate. Clayton stepped out and waved his arm over his head.

"Harry!"

He strapped Sabrina safely into the wheelchair before walking over to the gate and unlocking the padlock.

"Get ready, my old friend, I've come to take you," said Clayton, one hand resting on the open car door.

"Take me where?"

"To the cemetery."

"I thought you didn't approve."

"I don't. But you're my friend and if it means a lot to you, then it means a lot to me."

Harry's eyes filled with tears, and he glanced down at his feet.

"Thank you." His voice was a whisper.

He pushed open the gate then stepped aside as Clayton drove in.

Harry left his friend sitting on the veranda with Sabrina while he went inside to change.

"What about Sabrina?" he asked when he came out, changed out of his track suit bottoms and T-shirt into his one good pair of trousers and shirt.

"I've asked Mrs. Jones to come over the wall and watch her. Told her we won't be long. She loves the sound of her own voice and Sabrina's an excellent listener!"

As they reversed up the driveway and pulled out of the gate, Harry's heart was pounding. He was anxious about leaving Sabrina, though he knew she'd be in good hands. He'd slowly and patiently explained to her that he was going out with Uncle Clayton, and although he knew she didn't understand the words, she understood the soothing intonations in his voice.

Then he kissed her on her forehead, whispered he loved her, and turned to Clayton.

"I'm ready."

He rarely left the house, except to take his morning walk, and he realised, as they drove, that this was the first time he'd been in a car or been further away than their block in five years – since Clayton and Calvin had come that day to collect him from Denzel's house where he'd been living after being released from jail. He had so little memory of that time, so little memory of anything from that day. He sometimes wondered how it was possible he was still breathing, how his heart had carried on beating when Margot's had stopped.

"You OK, my old friend?" Clayton startled him back to the present.

"I'm OK."

"You sure you want to go through with this?"

"Yes."

And he slipped back into silence, watching the familiar yet different landscape pass him by and trying his best not to think about that day.

The cemetery was on the opposite end of town, not far from where Harry and Ruby had grown up. And as they drew closer, Harry's mind went back again to their childhood, and he remembered Clayton making the long bicycle ride out as a teenager, ostensibly to see his friend, but really to visit Ruby.

As if he could read his mind, Clayton turned to glance at him. "A long way to go to see an old friend." And the double meaning wasn't lost on either of them.

"You really had us going for a while there, you old rascal!" smiled Harry. "Pretending you were coming out to visit me when really it was Ruby."

"What?" laughed Clayton with mock indignation. "Surely after all these years you must have figured it out! I rode all the way out there for your mom's samosas!"

And they both chuckled.

At mention of his mother, Harry grew thoughtful again. He wondered if love was genetic: if members of one family were predisposed to being successful at love – or not. If so, he decided, his family collectively failed in that department. All except for Ruby, he supposed, and he glanced briefly at Clayton in the driver's seat and smiled to himself.

CHAPTER SIX

1922

RUDO'S FAMILY HAD hoped that would be the end of it. Tafadzwa had grabbed her wrist, barely noticing the spittle running down her chin or her heaving chest, breathless from the retching. He dragged her out of the alleyway and as she strained around to catch a glimpse of Ali, saw him lying motionless in the dirt, his head to one side, blood smeared across his temple.

Rudo was beaten by her father when Tafadzwa recounted the story. Then she was locked in her room with strict instructions that she only be allowed out to use the toilet. Her meals would be delivered to her.

She crumpled into a damp, weak heap in a corner of the room, hugging her knees to her chest. She was ill and afraid. What had happened to Ali? Was he dead? Was he badly injured? Was she ever going to see him again?

When the nausea bubbled again in her throat, there was no time to call out for someone to unlock the door and she vomited into a scarf. If Ali was dead, she thought, then she was better off dead too.

The vomiting was the first clue. The room was rich with the sweet stink when her mother came to unlock the door for dinner that day. She averted her eyes from Rudo's tear-streaked face.

Her lack of appetite was the second. Over the days that followed, her mother became certain what was wrong and had no choice but to talk to her husband.

He stormed into the room and threatened to beat her again if she didn't tell the truth, and once Rudo confessed she had had sex with the Indian boy, she was given exactly 10 minutes to gather her things from the room and leave. Her mother stood to one side and couldn't bring herself to meet her daughter's eyes.

Rudo packed her few belongings in an old flour sack and left, with no idea where she was going or how she would get there.

Ali had been badly bruised and beaten but, after about half an hour, was able to heave himself out of the dust and stumble home. He washed his wounds and lay in bed, weak and in agony for most of the weekend. By Monday morning he was stiff but able to take a slow, painful walk to work. He was spurred on by the hope of seeing Rudo; he had no idea what had happened to her after she was dragged out of the alleyway and his mind was in torment.

But she didn't come to work that day. Or the next. On the third day, he mustered up the courage to ask his boss.

"Is Rudo off sick?"

Mr. Patel looked up from his desk.

"Who?" his brow was furrowed.

"The cleaner," and his voice was tight as he said it.

"I fired her," he said with a toss of his hand, his attention back on the work on his desk.

Ali didn't know where she lived; he didn't even know her last name, he realised with horror. He walked the streets till late every night hoping to find her, but nothing.

He was lying in his darkened room after work, exhausted from the day at the shop and the relentless walking, looking for Rudo. He was hungry but too weak to get up and prepare something to eat. Then came the tentative knock. He pushed himself off the bed and limped to the door, opening it just a crack. And there, in the light of the doorway, was a glorious wedge of Rudo's face. He threw the door open and pulled her into his arms, burying his face in her soft, sweet neck.

They lay side-by-side on his narrow bed that first evening, his hand cupped over her belly, his head on her chest as she sang soft, sweet Shona melodies to him until they both drifted off to sleep.

The next morning, she was up early and had already started a small fire and made him a cup of tea and a bowl of porridge by the time he awoke. He gently scolded her, telling her she needed her rest, but couldn't hide his pleasure at being cared for by her.

He left for work with strict instructions that she take it easy, and almost ran home at the end of each day.

The first few weeks were bliss: they were together, and nothing and no-one else mattered.

But soon reality began to set in. They had nothing but a dusty room which barely contained a bed. And there was a baby coming. Ali approached Mr. Patel for a raise but word had got out that he was having a baby with the cleaning girl, and his boss barely looked at him when he told him there was no money. Ali knew his days with Mr. Patel were numbered.

He started searching for a new job but there was nothing. The Indians had black-balled him, news travelled fast in the small community, and Whites were reluctant to employ Indians when Blacks were willing to work for so much less.

Rudo tried to keep his spirits up, telling him it was going to be alright, but he became more and more anxious.

He knew Rudo would need to see a doctor at some stage; they would need to buy baby clothes and blankets, would eventually have a third mouth to feed.

He knew what he had to do. He mentioned it to Rudo one evening, discouraged and worn down by yet another futile day of job hunting.

She was afraid, but also knew they were short of options. They packed their meagre belongings and headed to Bulawayo.

Ali had never admired his big brother more. Mohammed answered the door and the first thing he did was let out a shout of happiness and clasp Ali in a bear hug.

To his credit, he only flinched a little when Rudo crept tentatively out of the shadows and in one glance he took in her round belly, her small, downturned face, the protective way in which Ali enclosed her in his arm.

It was decided that the first thing they would have to do was talk to Uncle Mustafa. Mohammed lived in a cramped one-bedroom apartment with his wife and a child of their own on the way. There was no room there for Ali and Rudo.

The reunion didn't go quite as well as the brothers'.

"Wallah!" shouted Uncle Mustafa, throwing his arms up in the air in horror when he opened the door and saw Ali standing next to Mohammed on his doorstep. His first instinct was to slap Ali hard around the head, then shout at him about family shame and betrayal.

But when Mohammed urged him to calm down and listen, he softened.

He loved the boys and knew, with the help of Allah, he could learn to forgive Ali. He wasn't prepared for the second blow: that Ali had come back with a pregnant girlfriend. And she was Black.

The shouting and slapping started afresh but, once again, Mohammed was able to quieten him and help him see reason.

"What's done is done, Uncle. He's my brother and he needs help. Allah would never want us to turn our back on the lost and downtrodden, and they don't get more lost than Ali."

Of that there was certainly no doubt, agreed Uncle Mustafa, and so, together, they hatched a plan.

Uncle Mustafa's generosity and tolerance did not extend to him being able to openly parade his nephew and pregnant Black girlfriend around the community. Maybe in time, but not now.

For now, he was willing to give Ali his old job back and provide him with a small room. But his relationship with Rudo must be kept secret.

Ali protested but, realising he was in no position to argue, eventually agreed.

He was to find Rudo accommodation at the other end

of town and although he could visit her, they could never be seen together in public.

Rudo was disheartened when she heard the plan, realising that they would be apart more than they would be together, but Ali reassured her he would visit all the time.

"But our love is not a thing to be ashamed of," she said.

"No, of course it's not, my love. And, in time, we'll convince them of that. But, for now, for the baby's sake, we have to do as they say. We have no choice."

Uncle Mustafa was, as always, good to Ali. He paid him a fair wage and, as the baby's birth drew closer, gave him a little extra to buy clothes and blankets.

Ali was grateful, and regretful that he'd caused the family pain. He was determined to make up for it by working hard and respecting their wishes to keep his relationship with Rudo under wraps.

When, at times, she complained about their separation, he urged her to be patient, convinced her it was what they had to do to secure their child's future.

Ali was not home when Rudo felt the first twinge of labour. Neither was he home when she felt her last. In desperation she had called the old woman from the main house who took matters in hand and helped her deliver her baby.

Once mother and baby were settled, the old woman extracted the address of the shop from Rudo and sent a message to Ali. His wife had given birth to a baby girl.

When the message arrived Ali, wide-eyed and breathless, approached Uncle Mustafa who immediately gave him permission to leave work. Just as Ali was running out the door he called him back, put one large hand on his nephew's shoulder and quietly slipped him a roll of money with the other.

"Congratulations, my boy. May Allah heap countless blessings on you and your family."

Ali smiled his thanks, but didn't trust his voice to speak.

He had thought it impossible to love Rudo any more than he did. Until he saw her lying on their bed, cradling their tightly swaddled baby. And as he sat beside her, enclosing his arms around her and their new-born daughter, Rudo closed her eyes, overcome with exhaustion and relief.

Ali had been so moved by the spirit with which his brother and Uncle had accepted him back into the family that he found himself re-connecting to his faith, knowing in his heart that it was Allah who had given them their pure motives.

He decided that their baby would have a Moslem name and be brought up in Islam. Rudo, having severed all ties to her family and culture and happy to have an anchor which could hold them all together, had no objection.

And so their little girl with her straight, black hair and coffee-coloured skin was named Leila – daughter of the night.

By the time Leila was one, her mother was attending Islamic lessons and covering her head in the traditional way. They learnt to say their Du'as, kneeling humbly on the ground and facing Mecca, preparing food using Halaal meat, bought from the only accredited Moslem butchery, situated half a day's walk on the other side of town.

Ali had taken to wearing a topi on his head and fervently attended Mosque, particularly on Fridays when special prayers were held.

But secrets don't stay hidden for long, particularly in a town the size of Bulawayo and, before long, everyone knew about Ali's "kafir" wife and Coloured child.

Ali endured his fair share of horrified looks but, for the most part, rode out the storm with uncharacteristic calm and patience; with time the scandal faded, overtaken in significance by fresh scandals, new gossip to occupy the women when they met in Jina's shop.

The renewed fervour with which he had approached his Faith had taught him humility and dignity, and when people saw his dedication and devotion, they were willing to give him a second chance.

Ali and Rudo were finally married in a small Nikkah at the Mosque attended by a handful of people. Their marriage was still not accepted by the authorities, but all that mattered to them was that they were accepted in the eyes of Allah.

They were free to mix with the community in open and even though Rudo was rarely invited to join the women in their social gatherings, she no longer had to hide.

Leila started attending Madressa and with her long, flowing hair and swarthy beauty, became a firm favourite among the uncles and aunties.

Mohammed was delighted to have his brother back and to see him embracing Islam again. Any misgivings he had had about Rudo were wiped away when he saw the positive influence she'd had on him. And he had a particularly soft spot for little Leila, almost the same age as his son, Jamal, and, over the years, one of his closest companions.

And so life went on in the blossoming little Moslem community. Ali toiled along with the rest of the men when the foundation for the first proper Mosque, close to the town centre, was dug; Rudo cleaned vegetables and cooked huge steel-bottomed pots of curry and rice along with the other women when prayers were held to bless the new site.

"Harry? Harry!"

"Yes?" startled out of his day dream about the past, Harry turned to the driver's seat to look at Clayton.

"We're here."

CHAPTER SEVEN

HARRY WASN'T SURE which was more difficult to see: Margot's name on the headstone or the words, "Beloved Wife and Mother". Where was the rest of her story?

Clayton had helped him locate the grave, treading through the long, unkempt grass while municipal workers sat watching them from the shade of a willow tree, grass slashers resting across their knees. In the early days the graves were more or less chronological but, with the war, order had given way to necessity.

It was hot, and both men had beads of sweat clinging to the back of their necks as they trudged through the labyrinth, each silently mouthing the names and the dates as they passed them.

Once they found it, a dark, granite headstone inscribed in white, Clayton saw his old friend crumple and grabbed his arm.

"I'm OK, I'm OK," whispered Harry and willed himself to stand back up.

"Are you sure?"

Harry nodded almost imperceptibly, not taking his eyes off the name.

"I'm going to go sit over there under the trees. Take your time. I'm here if you need me," said Clayton and he walked away, leaving his friend to his solitude and his pain.

Harry slowly removed the floppy hat from his head and held it with both hands to his chest, kneeling down slowly, one stiff leg at a time, at the foot of the grave.

Then he dropped his chin to his chest and allowed the tears, frozen inside him all these years, to run down his cheeks.

The last time he'd cried, he realised with alarm, was that day, kneeling over Margot's body, covered in her blood. Not so much a cry as a howl, he thought, a sound he could hear as if it was coming from somewhere outside of him, from someone – or something – else. Then they'd come to take him away – he tried to resist but was no match for the three policemen dragging him – and he stopped the howling, the crying, the speaking. He stopped.

More than anything that day, Harry wanted to be dead, cursing his heart which stubbornly kept beating when everything else inside him died.

His eyes still blinded with tears, he forced himself to conjure up an image of Margot far from that derelict lot and this dusty grave, and slowly, as his tears subsided and his breath returned to normal, he saw her.

Margot, hair held back with a paisley blue bandana which echoed the colour of her eyes, barefoot and kneeling in front of a flower bed that ran the length of the veranda, a gardening fork in her muddy hands. Emma and Peter on either side of her and laughing as she helped them plant seedlings of Namaqualand daisies. Every time she smiled over at Harry, preparing the soil for the seedlings as they worked, he could feel his heart grow too large for his chest, sense the arteries pumping faster to accommodate it. And the blood would rush to his face and he'd feel the warm summer day grow even hotter on his cheeks.

And Margot would smile a little more.

The daisies blossomed brighter than the sun that year, their burnished yellow and orange faces turned up towards the blue sky. It was the school holidays and the children would run out early each morning, the dew still bright on the lawn, and check their progress. They were responsible for weeding and, under Harry's instruction, watering. They'd carry their mother's bright pink watering can, which Emma would laughingly say looked like a giant tea pot, to the tap at the front of the garden. With Harry's help, they'd set the spout under the tap, fill it and carry it to the flower bed. Then they'd take turns to water, Harry gently tilting the spout to create a light sprinkle.

Peter had all the patience in the world, allowing Harry's hand to guide him, and controlling the water so it came out in a light, steady flow. But Emma always wanted to do it all by herself and, in her enthusiasm, would tip the can down too hard and dump the water in a big splash at the foot of the flowers, splattering her bare toes with mud.

Harry never grew impatient, but would gently level the can up and help her to try again. Margot would be inside doing the morning chores, but come out regularly to check on them, or to bring them warm cups of sweet tea which the children would drink sitting on a blanket on the lawn, and which she and Harry would sip while leaning against the veranda wall as they talked.

This was on the days David was away fighting in the

war, and Harry was staying on the property to watch the family. Before David came home on leave and Harry was despatched home to Gwennie and the children. And he felt again the pain and the guilt.

When David came home on leave that particular time, the daisies, like the school holidays, were coming to an end and had started to wilt and wane. Harry had barely opened the gate to allow David to drive in, and he was being admonished.

"I go away and everything falls to wrack and ruin! Look at the state of this garden! What the hell have you been doing while I've been away, boy? Clean this mess up before you knock off," he said, sweeping a dismissive hand over the daisies before striding indoors. Harry could hear Margot and David's raised voices as he started on the task.

Peter and Emma were heartbroken watching their beloved flower bed dug up, but Harry took time to show them how he was gathering up the seeds and would store them in a warm, dry place till next season when they would plant them again.

"They're not dead," Harry had smiled as he stored the seeds carefully away in a terracotta pot behind his little room. "They're just resting and will come back even bigger and more beautiful when we plant them next year."

Of course none of them knew there would be no next year, no next season, and Harry, still kneeling at the foot of Margot's grave, thought the pain in his chest may suffocate him.

CHAPTER EIGHT

BY THE TIME Clayton stood up from the spot he'd found under the willow trees and walked over to his friend, Harry was sitting back on his haunches, worn out with emotion.

"Come, my old friend," he said softly, kneeling down beside him, "I think it's time to go. Sabrina will be waiting."

Hearing Sabrina's name gave him the strength to slowly drag himself from his thoughts and allow Clayton to help him to his feet. Then the two men walked slowly back to the car, neither of them saying a word.

They were silent all the way back to the house, Clayton glancing over every now and again to check on his friend who was looking straight ahead, his hands folded in his lap.

Clayton pulled up to the gate and switched off the engine, and then turned to face him.

"How are you doing? I'm beginning to think maybe this was a big mistake."

"It wasn't a mistake, Clay, I had to go, I had to see her just one more time." And his voice broke as he said it.

Clayton put a hand on his friend's shoulder and could feel his thin frame shudder as he tried to control his ragged breathing.

Finally, Harry's breath returned to normal and Clayton removed his hand.

"If you're sure you're OK, I'm going to head home. Ruby's going to be wondering where I am, and I'm sure Sabrina is missing you."

Harry nodded.

"I'm fine, I'm really fine. Thank you, this has meant more to me than you can ever know," he said, opening the door as he said it. Then he shut the car door and walked slowly towards the gate.

As Clayton reversed and started to drive away, he glanced back one more time and saw Harry standing on the other side of the gate, waving goodbye.

Harry walked slowly down the long driveway, lost in his own thoughts, and didn't see Talia and Calvin standing on the veranda watching him until he was a couple of metres away. Sabrina was sitting in the wheelchair under the awning and out of the sun.

"Where the fuck were you?" Calvin said, walking towards him, his green eyes dark with emotion.

"I went out…with Clayton."

"You went out? Just like that? And left Sabrina?" Talia's voice was rising.

"She wasn't alone, Clayton arranged for Mrs. Jones to watch her."

"Where the fuck were you?" Calvin repeated.

"There was somewhere I needed to go, that's all. Clayton offered to take me." Harry's voice withered.

"Where?" And this time Calvin's voice was lead.

"The cemetery," said Harry under his breath.

"What?"

"The cemetery." He said it a little louder this time.

"The cemetery?" Calvin's brow furrowed. "The cemetery," he repeated, rolling the word around in his mouth. And then, slowly, realisation dawned. He took a step forward and looked his father square in the eye.

"You fucking went to her grave!" Calvin's voice was low and deadly. "What the fuck is wrong with you? How many more people have to die before you give up? What the fuck is wrong with you?" he repeated.

Harry shrank.

"Calvin…" Talia took a step forward and placed a cautionary hand on her brother's arm. He threw his arm in the air, flinging hers away, not taking his eyes off Harry.

"Wasn't it enough for you? Fucking up our family, fucking up Ma – for her? When the fuck is it enough?" Calvin was yelling now and Harry took a step back and put his hands out in front of him.

"Son…"

"Don't you fuckin' 'son' me! What son? What the fuck do you care? What do you care about any of us – anything? The only thing you cared about was her and hers, we didn't even feature. If she hadn't died you would've fucked off with her – fucked off and left us without a second thought! No, the only thing you fucking cared about was yourself – always did and always will!" Calvin lifted his hand, then stopped himself mid-way and dropped it to his side.

His shoulders slumped and the life seemed to seep out of him.

"Calvin, please…" Harry put his hand on his arm but Calvin just slowly shook his head and walked away, kicking a deck chair on the edge of the veranda before disappearing towards the back.

CHAPTER NINE

1933

THE FIRST SIGN of trouble was soon after Leila turned 10. It was a little game she played with her father: when it was time for him to come home, she'd run to the corner and wait for him. The moment he rounded the street, she would plummet down the grassy verge and fling herself into his arms.

She was getting to be a tall, gangly-limbed pre-pubescent, but Ali would still grab her in his arms and toss her up so she could hug him tightly around the neck.

He knew she would outgrow their little routine eventually and wanted to hold on to it as long as possible.

But nowadays when Leila spotted her father coming around the corner, he wasn't walking briskly as he used to do, he wasn't craning his neck to spot his little girl.

He was slower, quieter, his feet shuffled as he walked; he lifted Leila with effort and she knew it wasn't because she was becoming too heavy.

Rudo noticed her husband's increasing lethargy and tried a few home remedies: natural glucose for renewed energy, sorghum porridge for strength, but nothing seemed to help.

Finally, she urged him to see a doctor.

Ali was diagnosed with TB and Rudo watched helplessly as he coughed himself breathless every night, soaked through with sweat by the following morning, too weak to raise his head. He began to dissolve before their eyes, his lanky frame shrunken down to nothing but a thin layer of skin, like plastic clinging to meat after it's been vacuum-packed. The once bright light in his green eyes slowly started to fade.

Almost exactly six months after the diagnosis, in the middle of a dark, cold winter's night, Rudo watched by the light of a paraffin lamp as he coughed for the last time, watched as he struggled to catch his breath – but there was none left to catch. And her beloved Ali died in her arms.

After prayers, led by an openly-weeping Mohammed and Uncle Mustafa, Ali's body was taken from the house to the Moslem section of the cemetery. The women stayed behind to pray and mourn, comforting arms wrapped around Rudo and Leila who sat like empty shells, too shocked and bereaved to cry.

Being a woman and not being allowed to go to the gravesite and see her beloved Ali laid to rest was the hardest thing Rudo had ever done and, for the first time, she regretted swapping her religion with another. These women felt like strangers, all she wanted was to see Ali, to hear his soothing voice, to see him walk through the door at the end of a long day and know that whatever problems there were in the world, it would be fine with him by her side.

She glanced across at her little girl, feisty and strong, her veins coursing with Ali's hot blood, and she felt afraid.

Mohammed and Uncle Mustafa were faithful to Ali's memory and stood by his young family. They set up a trust fund for Leila's education and together raised money to give Rudo a small living allowance. She looked for a job, finally finding work in the kitchen of a small takeaway restaurant where the hours were long and the conditions harsh, but at least she had some money coming in.

Leila was alone in the small apartment much of the time, although Mohammed would often call for her so she could play with her cousins.

But as she grew to be a teenager, the differences between them started to become more apparent. There were the little jibes from others calling her "little blackie", there were the questions she had about her mother's family, why no one ever spoke about her gogo or baba.

Rudo was worked off her feet and often too busy and impatient to answer all her questions. She was also hesitant to open up old wounds, closed for so many years and too painful to face.

The more she fobbed Leila off, the more persistent she became.

"But why don't we see my grandmother?" she'd insist.

"I've told you, Leila, because she's all the way in Cape Town and it's very far away."

"No, I mean your mom. Why don't we see that grandmother?"

"It's a long story Leila and I don't have time right now."

"You never have time, Ma. I'm not going to stop asking. I really want to know."

When Leila was 15, Rudo finally decided she was old enough to know the truth. After work one Monday evening she sat her daughter down next to her and told her the story of how she and Ali met, how they fell in love, how her parents didn't approve and sent her away, skirting over the sordid details and watching as the expression in Leila's huge eyes changed from wonder to outrage.

"It's ancient history, Leila, so long ago it's best forgotten, but I could see you couldn't let it go, so there you have it, now you know," said Rudo when she came to the end.

"It's not ancient history, Ma. It's my history," was all that Leila said that night.

If Rudo hadn't been so preoccupied with her job, if she'd taken time to reflect on Leila's determined personality, she would have known it wouldn't end there.

But the last thing she expected was the letter that arrived the following month.

It was a few simple lines on grey manila paper, enclosed in a brown envelope with a window, the address scrawled untidily in the upper left-hand corner.

Dear Rudo,

I have asked Phineas to write this for me. We have received the photograph and letter from Leila and would be happy if she came to visit us. Your father has not been well for some time and will not put up any protest.

Your mother

Rudo reeled. It had been over 15 years since she'd had any contact with her family, since they'd sent her away, discarded her as if she were dead – no, worse than dead. And now, after all these years, this.

Her first reaction was anger.

"How did you even find the address?" she shouted.

Leila looked down at her feet.

"I went through your bedside drawer. It was on one of your old identity papers. I hoped it hadn't changed after all these years, I just took a chance."

"You went through my personal things, my private things?"

Leila looked up sharply. "Ma, I'm not going to apologise for that. They're my family too."

Rudo didn't know what else to say.

Her next reaction was fear, fear that, like Ali, she would somehow lose Leila.

She tried, through the tears and the shouting, to explain this to Leila but all the young girl could think of was meeting her mother's family, trying to find a way to reconnect to the roots which had been hacked away before she'd even been born. She was desperate to find out where she fitted in, where she belonged. She was quite sure it wasn't here, in this small Moslem community where her skin colour, her hair, her accent, her mother, were all so different to everyone else's.

Finally, Rudo realised there was no dissuading her – Leila would go to Salisbury with or without her mother's approval. Rudo had been her age when she'd chosen her own path, she didn't want to push Leila to break the ties from her in the same way.

"I can see you're determined and that no amount of talking sense to you is going to work," Rudo said at last. "But you won't go alone, I'm coming with you."

So Rudo asked for a week's leave from the restaurant and the pair set off by train for Salisbury. She told no-one but

Mohammed where they were going and although he wasn't comfortable with the plan and expressed his worry to her, he understood why they had to go and gave them his blessing.

"Perhaps, my dear Rudo, it's time for us to put the ugliness of the past behind us and ask Allah to help us forgive those who pained us. Leila reminds me so much of Ali, headstrong, determined, willing to fight for what she believes. Pray Allah gives her the wisdom and the patience too."

Rudo felt tears spring to her eyes at the mention of her beloved Ali and, boarding the train the next day, Mohammed's words were still ringing in her ears.

It was the longest journey of her life. The economy class was cramped and airless, seven people squeezed onto a wooden bench designed for four. It lurched and shook uncontrollably, smoke from the steam engine pouring in through the windows, streaked black with coal.

But Leila didn't complain once, not even when a woman holding a baby under one arm and a live chicken under the other, squeezed herself in between them and, without even asking, handed her the baby to hold.

Within minutes she had the crying, squirming child sitting calmly in her arms and Rudo marvelled once again at all the ways in which her daughter continued to surprise and amaze her.

CHAPTER TEN

A WEEK LATER when Rudo boarded the same train, this time bound for Bulawayo, she was alone. Leila and her grandmother had accompanied her to the train station and stood waving to her as the train lumbered away, encompassed in a cloud of smoke.

She waved until they were out of sight and then, finally, leaned against the greasy window and closed her eyes.

A week earlier Rudo's heart had been thumping uncontrollably in her chest as they'd approached the town of Salisbury, a sprawling capital city in the making. After a 15-year absence it was almost unrecognisable to her, a foreign land.

It took some time for her to find her way to her parents' home, it had been so long and the area was so changed.

Built to keep the Black neighbourhoods separate from the White, Coloured and Indian, her township, like all the others, was over-populated and underdeveloped.

The only thing that distinguished one squalid house from the other was the black house number painted crudely on the side of the wall.

People stared at them wherever they went: the dark woman, her head covered by a scarf, not tied in the traditional way at the nape of her neck but under her chin, trousers worn under her dress; the young girl with the long, black hair and cocoa coloured skin who walked beside her. They stared even harder when Rudo opened her mouth to speak, her native Shona sounding distant and foreign on her lips after all these years.

After asking countless directions they finally found the house: number 68711. The house looked smaller than she remembered, grey and sad. A tiny patch of mealies rustled in the slight breeze.

They opened the small, rusty gate, barely hanging on to its hinges, and it screeched in protest. A face appeared at the small, high window facing the driveway.

Rudo clasped Leila's hand and held it tightly, as much for the young girl's comfort and reassurance as her own. Then she adjusted her head scarf and walked determinedly up the short, rocky pathway to the front door.

There was no need to knock. As Rudo lifted her hand, the door was thrust open and there stood a tall, skinny boy about 17 years old. The shock hit her like a bolt: this was her little brother Tendai.

How do you greet a brother you haven't seen for 15 years? A boy who was two years old when you left, who probably has no memory of you? Rudo wasn't sure. She stepped forward unsteadily and saw her hesitation reflected in his eyes. Then in a kind of fumble they fell into each other's arms and hugged. Rudo felt the huge sense of loss press on her chest and she struggled, for a moment, to breathe.

She pulled away slightly to look at him, and then she saw her mother standing quietly in the darkness just beyond the doorway.

Leaving her brother's side, she walked slowly over and took the old woman in her arms. Her mother was openly crying, the blanket which was wrapped around her shoulders falling to the ground as she clutched her daughter.

Rudo realised in that moment how hard it must have been for her mother to let her go, how, in the traditional way, she had followed her husband's wishes to protect the family from shame but had regretted it every single day. How she'd spent her days and nights wondering how her daughter was, praying she was healthy and happy and didn't cry as much for her mother as her mother cried for her.

How Rudo had longed for her mother's comfort and guidance when, just a child herself, she'd given birth to a baby and had to fumble her way to motherhood all on her own. Through all those hard years, trying to win acceptance from the community, living with rejection and uncertainty and then losing Ali, how she would have loved to have her mother by her side.

When they finally let go of each other Rudo motioned for Leila to come forward and she introduced her daughter to her mother. The old woman began to cry afresh.

Just then there was a deep groaning from somewhere inside the dark house and Rudo stiffened.

Wordlessly, her mother gently took her arm and led her down the short, dark passageway to the second bedroom, at the end of the house.

Standing on the threshold of the tiny room, it took a few minutes for her eyes to adjust to the darkness, and then she saw a small bundle on the bed, blankets piled high.

She walked uncertainly over and knelt by her father's side, her head bowed. When she raised her eyes to look at him she hardly recognised the shrunken head, the sunken eyes, the little remaining hair on his head grey and grizzled.

This was the hulking, powerful man who'd paralysed her with fear, whose booming voice had made her tremble. Where was his power now?

Her father turned his head vaguely in her direction and tried to raise his head. But the effort exhausted and drained him and he slumped back down, groaning again.

"I salute you, my father," said Rudo, her voice thin.

He groaned again then squeezed his eyes shut. Rudo sat a few moments longer before slowly standing up and leaving the room.

Her mother and Leila were in the kitchen and when she reached the doorway, she paused to watch them together. The tall, willowy girl with long, jet black hair standing beside the old woman, her heavy frame made bulkier by the thick blanket tied around her waist. They stood looking at each other, their fingers almost touching, a strange shadow of resemblance between them. Rudo didn't want to interrupt the moment but the pair sensed her presence and looked towards the doorway; her daughter smiled beatifically at her and mouthed "Thank you."

CHAPTER ELEVEN

THERE WERE SEVEN people living in the tiny two-bedroomed house. With Rudo and Leila there were nine of them, almost every available square of floor space taken up in the evenings when blankets were laid out to make up the beds.

Apart from her parents and Tendai there was her cousin, Phineas, and his three children aged between three and 11. Phineas had lost his wife at childbirth three years earlier and had lived with Rudo's parents ever since.

Although it made the house crowded, Rudo's mother was grateful for the company and the help.

"I don't know how I would have managed without Phineas, your father being as he is," she told Rudo that first evening as they sat drinking tea from enamel mugs after the dinner had been cleared away.

"How long has he been like this?"

"Five years. It gets worse every year."

"What's wrong?"

"Broken body, broken heart. Old age, my child, like me."

"You're not old, mother, you're amazing, you still look so well, you are, aren't you?" she said, suddenly panicked.

"No, child I'm well, I'm strong. I have to be. I have no choice."

One of Rudo's main concerns was how they were going to keep the Moslem laws while staying with her family.

The first night she refused to let Leila eat the meat in the stew and, despite her mother's protests, dished up only sadza and vegetables.

"We can't, Ma, it's not Halaal," she tried to explain.

"What is this Halaal? Our meat is suddenly not good enough for you?" said her mother, her hands on her hips and clicking her tongue.

Rudo eventually gave up trying to explain.

At the end of the meal, she and Leila retired to her mother's bedroom and did their prayers and, in the morning, she set out just after dawn in search of a Moslem butchery.

Her family's sometimes quizzical, sometimes disapproving looks followed their every move.

Rudo was beginning to notice that Leila's faith was waning, as if her heart wasn't in it anymore. She would only pray when her mother told her to and seemed to have lost the religious ardour she'd once had. Rudo wondered what had happened to the little girl who had always been top of the class in Madressa, who would say the prayers with such feeling, learning the Arabic sutras as fluently as her spoken English. Islam, besides being their chosen faith, was their link to Ali.

She tried talking to her about it but Leila was evasive. And now with her grandmother always by her side, Rudo felt outnumbered.

The two had become inseparable; Leila would follow her grandmother wherever she went, sitting with her in the kitchen while she prepared vegetables, following her around the small yard when she went outside to tend to the scant beds, helping her prepare food over the open fire at the back.

It was as if Leila was trying to make up for lost time, soak in as much of her grandmother as she could, hanging on to her every word, even though she understood so little of the language, staring at her as if she was afraid she might vanish from her life again.

By the end of their one-week stay the inevitable happened. Leila wanted to stay. And Rudo was powerless in the face of her family and their obvious love and attachment to her daughter.

"We haven't seen her for 15 years. We have to spend time with her now, teach her our ways, fasten the link that ties us."

So it was decided that Leila would stay, although only for a month, Rudo insisted.

But even as she set off back to Bulawayo and the train belched thick, black smoke as it steamed down the track, the image of the old woman and the young girl becoming more and more distant and then disappearing altogether, Rudo knew, as any mother knows her daughter's heart, that she had lost Lelia.

One month became two, then three and, eventually, six. Leila wrote regularly to her mother and her letters were always the same: how happy she was in Salisbury living with her grandmother, but how much she missed Rudo and wished her mother would come and live with them. Then, wrote Leila, her life would be complete.

But Rudo couldn't see herself moving back to her old life and losing her link to the laws of Islam and Ali's family which had become such an intrinsic part of who she was. And when she heard how happy Leila was, she knew she couldn't force her to come back either.

After six months Leila came home to Bulawayo, travelling with an older male cousin. But it was only to visit with her mother and pack up the last of her things.

The first thing Rudo noticed was that her daughter no longer wore trousers under her dress and her legs were exposed. The second thing she noticed was how tall she'd grown.

After that visit, Rudo would see Leila only about once a year. On the occasions when she came to Bulawayo, Rudo would try to talk to her about her faith, try to encourage her to come pray with her or attend meetings in the women's section of the Mosque. But Leila always had an excuse.

Finally, when Rudo pushed her a little harder, Leila blurted it out.

She had decided to become a Catholic.

"Why, Leila, why turn your back on our faith, on the faith of your dear father? It's a betrayal of his name, his memory!" said Rudo.

"Would daddy have wanted me to live a lie, Ma? I don't think so. I'm old enough now to choose and I have chosen to be a Catholic. I don't mean to hurt you with this, please don't cry, but I feel it in my heart that this is where my path lies."

Rudo had no choice but to accept her daughter's wishes, though her heart was breaking.

She reacted by becoming even more devout, praying constantly, spending all her free time working for the women's Islamic society, helping out at the Madressa.

By the time Rudo was an elderly woman she had a reputation as one of the most faithful followers of Islam in the Bulawayo community, a stalwart who had helped build the Mosque up to its present-day glory. Even those who had once treated her like an outcast, viewed her with quiet respect and reverence. And her story of conversion was a favourite among the elders when illustrating the all-encompassing, all-transforming power of Allah's love.

Leila met Lawrence Rhoades when she was 19. He saw her at a church dance and was immediately struck by her distinctive looks, so hard to place, so difficult to forget.

Neither her grandmother nor her mother was surprised when she announced she was dating a Coloured man, they'd always imagined she would attract and marry someone mixed, like herself.

Their one concern was that Lawrence was a lot older than Leila, almost 20 years older when he asked for her hand in marriage.

"What's wrong with him? Why has he waited so long to marry?" asked her grandmother.

"Don't sound so suspicious, Gogo, it's nothing sinister. He says he's been waiting for the right woman."

"And I suppose you think you are that woman?" she clicked her tongue and folded her arms across her ample bosom.

"Gogo, of course I am!" said Leila, her eyes twinkling.

And her grandmother couldn't help but smile along with her – as this beloved grandchild of hers always made her do.

Leila and Lawrence married and had two children, Harry and Rihanna.

Rihanna, her second born, was her one concession to the memory of her late father's faith, the only thing that still linked her to her Moslem roots. As she cradled her baby girl in her arms the night she was born, leaning down to kiss her round, dimpled, ruby cheeks, she hoped her father was looking down at her with love, and not disappointment.

Harry would tell Sabrina the story as he pushed her in the wheelchair up and down the driveway. "That was your Granny Ruby, my girl," and he would lean down as he said it and kiss her on her smooth, round forehead.

CHAPTER TWELVE

1953

WHEN HARRY TURNED 10, two very distinct events took place: his father left and his great grandmother, Nani Sharifa, came to visit from Cape Town.

Until then, Gogo Rudo had been the only grandmother they'd known, a strict but loving woman who'd come to stay with them for a couple of months at a time, often during the school holidays when she could watch the children while their mother was at work. Gogo Rudo could use a wooden spoon to stir her famous chicken curry as effectively as she could use it on their bottoms – and the children were treated to equal measures of both.

At least a month before she arrived, preparations would begin to transform their home into a Halaal household. All pork products would be used up and any trace of Lawrence's Viceroy brandy whisked away.

So when they heard that their Nani was coming to visit all the way from Cape Town, and that she too was Moslem, they knew the drill.

They wondered what this new, mystical granny from all the way across the seas would be like.

Ruby had asked if she had a beard like Gogo Rudo, and Leila had shushed her.

"Don't be rude, Ruby Rhoades!"

"It was just a question," she pouted.

Harry asked if she liked to play spear grass wars, and Leila had clicked her tongue impatiently.

Leila couldn't have answered if she'd tried. She knew nothing about her grandmother on her father's side. Rudo had spoken only a little about her, stories Ali had recounted of the tiny woman with the heart of gold who he'd left in Cape Town as a 15-year-old boy and never seen again.

When news that Ali was having a child with a Black woman first reached his parents in Cape Town, Ali's father had threatened to disown him.

"He's no son of mine!" he'd raged – or so Sharifa's Auntie Yasmin would tell him, years later, when she visited the family in Bulawayo.

"Why can't he understand this is Ali's choice, that as long as he loves her that's all that matters," Sharifa had told her aunt "He will always be our son, our Ali."

She'd tried to make her husband see sense, tried to reconcile the family, but he wouldn't have it and only grew more angry. Auntie Yasmin had dropped her eyes and said no more, but Ali remembered his father's temper and his heart ached.

When he received news that his father had died of cancer – Leila was five at the time – he felt nothing but a sense of anger that he had never accepted Rudo, or his beautiful little girl.

Ali's mother had started writing to him soon after her husband died, simple, short letters written very slowly with a shaky hand.

My darling Ali

Forgive me for my poor writing, I am learning slowly and trying to do a bit more every day to become better. I heard little Leila is five now, Ma Shaa Allah. May Allah bless her and keep her safe. I am well. Since the death of your father, I have taken in a tenant, a sweet young woman named Marriyam. She helps with the household expenses and the chores and is a wonderful companion to me. Auntie Yasmin and Uncle Sameer live next door and they take good care of me and I am happy. Greet your wife from me. Should Allah will it, we will meet again one day.

I love you, my son.

Ma

She would write about once every three months and Ali would reply, sending money when he could, as well as photographs of Rudo and Leila.

Little Leila has grown so big and so beautiful, Ma Shaa Allah! Greet your wife for me. His mother would write.

When Ali died, the letters, always addressed to him but including a greeting for Rudo, stopped.

Relatives said her heart was so broken by the loss of her beloved Ali that she locked herself in her room for a week, refusing food or water until, finally, Auntie Yasmin had to practically force-feed her.

Rudo heard nothing from her for over 10 years, but when Mohammed and his family visited her in Cape Town a couple of years later, she sent a turquoise blue silk shawl for Leila and a pair of shell earrings for Rudo.

And then, out of the blue, a letter.

Dear Rudo

How are you and my dear Leila? I am writing because I am now an old woman and I don't know how many more years Allah will spare me. My one heart's desire is to see my granddaughter, Leila, before I die – if I can find safe passage to Bulawayo, and if you'll have me.

Sharifa

It took almost 15 years for Sharifa's wish to come true, and even as an old man many years later, Harry remembered the day she arrived as vividly as if it was yesterday.

His great Uncle Mohammed's blue Ford Anglia pulled up at the gate and the children ran to the gate to meet him. Uncle Mohammed always gave the best hugs – and the best sweets.

He waved a big hand out the window at them and drove in. He stepped out of the car and came around to the passenger door and opened it, reaching in with his hand to help his passenger.

A little old woman with a grey plait of hair snaking down her bent back got out, swinging one leg slowly onto the ground followed by the other and then straightening up as best she could. She was wearing a black and silver shalwar kameez, a matching black shawl draped over her shoulders. She lifted the scarf over her head and covered her hair, flinging one length over each shoulder and tucking them snugly in.

She had Ruby's shy, dimpled smile, and she shone it on them now as she opened her arms wide. The children ran to her, and she wrapped her arms around both of them at once, kissing the tops of their warm heads and holding them tight, and they stood like that for what seemed like a long time.

CHAPTER THIRTEEN

NANI SHARIFA WAS still standing in the driveway hugging Harry and Ruby tightly in her arms when Leila came out, holding the door open as she hesitated in the doorway.

Sharifa slowly unfurled her arms from around the children and looked up, resting a hand on each of their shoulders. The two women stood looking at each other across the expanse of time and distance that had separated them, and then, still clasping the children close, Sharifa started to walk slowly towards her on bent legs.

Leila took a step forward then stopped, mesmerised by the strange familiarity of the old woman's smile, her father's smile. Another moment's hesitation and she rushed forward; the two women hugged, the children between them.

Then Sharifa straightened as best she could, reached up and cupped Leila's face with her hands.

"My Leila, you are so much like your dear father, my Ali, Ma Shaa Allah," said Sharifa in a shaky voice, and she gently pulled her down towards her, kissing her granddaughter on the forehead and then on each cheek, before placing her temple against hers and closing her eyes and whispering a prayer of thanks under her breath.

The children, bored already by all the sentiment, were running around them and playing, Harry chasing the dusty hens around with a stick and Ruby shrieking with laughter behind him. Sharifa and Leila slowly pulled apart and, holding her grandmother's left hand in her right, Leila looked over at Mohammed who'd been watching them and smiling.

"Uncle Mohammed," she whispered.

"My sweet Leila," he replied walking up and kissing her on each cheek. "Now the circle is complete. Ali must be looking down on us from Jannah and smiling." And with an arm around each of the women, he walked them slowly into the house.

The reunion with Rudo, later that day, was not so spontaneously affectionate. Leila stood at the wood stove where she was preparing dinner and looked over at the two women sitting stiffly beside each other, and wondered who would be the first to thaw.

Leila thought it ironic how much mother-in-law and daughter-in-law shared, despite the outward distance between them: heads covered in the same way, hands folded in their laps the same way, and, as dinner was served, both spontaneously closing their eyes and holding out their hands, palms facing up, muttering the meal time blessing, bismillah-ir-rahman-ir-rahim, 'in the name of God, the gracious, the merciful', under their breaths.

They both poked at the meat and waited for Leila to confirm it was Halaal, and, after eating, they both pushed back their chairs and retreated to opposite ends of the house for Maghrib: praise be to Allah who has fed us and given us drink and made us Moslem.

It had been arranged that Rudo would stay over for a few

days and that night, lying in bed next to Leila, she struggled to sleep, clutching the blanket to her chest and staring up at the dark ceiling.

When Leila rolled over in the night and saw her mother lying beside her, her eyes wide open, she raised herself sleepily up on her elbow and looked across at her.

"What's going on, Ma?" her voice was thick with sleep.

"Nothing, Leila, go back to sleep."

"How can I sleep with you lying there wide awake?"

"I'm sorry, my girl, I didn't mean to wake you."

"What's wrong, Ma?"

She was surprised to see her steely mother's eyes fill with tears.

"So much lost, and I don't know how to get it back."

"We can't get it back, Ma. But we can make sure we don't keep losing. Daddy wouldn't have wanted that."

Rudo sighed and rolled over onto her side to look at her daughter. "You've turned into a wise and beautiful woman. Your father would be so proud of you."

And she ran her fingers through Leila's dark hair before finally closing her eyes and falling into a restless sleep.

"Mohammed has told me you are on the burial committee," said Sharifa as she and Rudo sat down to breakfast together on the first day. "And on the charity committee."

"The wedding committee too," said Rudo, not looking up from her bowl of porridge.

Sharifa nodded, her fingertips resting lightly on the table. "You are a credit to our family, Rudo, to Ali's memory."

Rudo looked up sharply.

"You look surprised to hear me say that, and I can understand why. We did not welcome you into the family as we should have. Things were different back then, so much more difficult. And my husband…"

"Things haven't changed much, I'm still viewed with suspicion by those who don't know me. But I had hoped my family, Ali's family, would be different."

Sharifa looked down.

"Words seem so inadequate in trying to tell you how sorry I am for the pain we caused you. I have made many mistakes in my life, and as time has gone on I have come to realise what really matters and what does not. I have been humbled, my dear Rudo, in the eyes of my fellow man and in the eyes of my creator. And my heart has broken more than once. I am not worthy of forgiveness, but I humbly ask you to find it in your heart to forgive me anyway."

Rudo didn't reply, and sat for a long time looking down at her hands lying in her lap and not saying a word. Then she sighed and put her hand on her mother-in-law's arm and the two women sat there for a long time, both too full of emotion to speak.

Leila came in to clear the breakfast dishes some time later and smiled to see the pair sitting together, Sharifa's hand resting on Rudo's as they talked about Ali.

She smiled again later when Rudo hauled the photo albums out of storage and the two of them sat side-by-side on the sofa paging through photographs, Sharifa trying to catch up on the last 30 years in one morning, a handkerchief in her hand to dab away the pool of tears that kept gathering in the wrinkled corners of her eyes.

“My beautiful boy, Ma Shaa Allah,” said Sharifa, running a finger gently over a photo of Ali, standing with arms crossed on his chest and laughing.

“His laughter was always so easy,” said Rudo. “No matter how bad things got, he never stopped laughing.” And Sharifa smiled a sad smile and quickly turned the page.

CHAPTER FOURTEEN

The Malay Quarters, Cape Town 1901

SHARIFA HAD OFTEN wondered how it felt, that kind of love. The kind that seemed to simultaneously shrink and expand your heart. Reduce you to your barest existence while making you feel like a colossus. She wished she'd had a chance to talk to her mother about it, that she hadn't died before she was old enough to ask, and she missed her now more than ever.

She looked down at Mohammed lying asleep in her arms, his lashes cresting his long, almond shaped eyes, and wondered if it felt a bit like this. Maybe in some ways, she thought, but she knew it had to feel greatly different too.

Sharifa had thought she might feel it when she married her husband. It didn't have the makings of a great romance, it's true. But her aunties had sat her down the night before her Mehndi and explained how it would be. How you didn't have to love them at first, how love could grow. How the husband who started out as a stranger, could become a lover (they giggled behind their hands at the word) – and even a friend.

They'd winked at her, and told her it would be wonderful, that she'd found a good man from a good family, Alhamdulillah, and they would bear children who would love her and worship Allah, and the cycle would continue to the end that had no end.

Then they gave her some tips about the wedding night, and the giggling had started afresh, turning into peals of raucous laughter as the night wore on.

Sharifa thought perhaps it was her fault she hadn't fallen in love with her husband. That she'd been stubborn and hard-hearted at the start. You see, the first thing she noticed about him, her head bent towards the ground, were his scuffed and dirty black shoes. And she had no explanation for the unreasonable disappointment and anger that washed over her. She'd spent the last 24 hours preparing for this day, bathing and waxing in the traditional way, her hair and skin oiled, being primped and preened by a cohort of aunties, all clucking around her, offering silk scarves and floral fragrances and more wedding night advice. She'd stood in front of the mirror afterwards, her aunties forming a half moon behind her and, for the first time in her life, imagined she caught a glimpse of the beauty people always credited her with, but she'd never been able to see herself. Her fair skin was glowing, deeply contrasting her jet-black hair, glossy from the coconut treatments and falling in a thick, rich mass to her shoulders. Her dark eyes were rimmed with kohl and the lashes – those perfect lashes – were long and curled. The dimples in her cheeks deepened as she smiled.

The aunties had nodded happily at their handiwork and chubby Auntie Bibi, her upper lip glistening with sweat, clicked her tongue in satisfaction. Then they'd covered Sharifa's hair with a luminous gold scarf – a gift to be unwrapped by her husband when they were finally alone, Auntie Yasmin had whispered with a smile – and threaded their arms through hers and walked her down the block to the tiny Mosque with its painted minaret where the Nikkah would take place.

Sharifa had kept her head down, catching glimpses of the neighbourhood children's bare feet as they ran up and down the cobblestone path alongside the wedding party, whooping with joy and skipping back and forth, and heard snatches of the quiet prayers for protection Auntie Bibi muttered under her breath as they walked and the calls of good wishes from the elderly men and women who sat on chairs outside their tiny front doors, watching the world pass by. Her heart was pounding. Was this how love felt?

The bride and groom had sat separately during the ceremony, as was traditional, and only afterwards was she presented to him. And now here she was looking down at a pair of ugly brogues sitting beside her, and her eyes filled unexpectedly with tears. Behind the veil and with her head down, no one could see her, and those scuffed, dirty shoes became blurry through the tears and dissolved in front of her. Eventually she looked away altogether, keeping her eyes fixed instead on her hands folded in her lap, so beautifully and painstakingly-painted with henna at the Mehndi, like delicate lace gloves covering the back of her narrow hands and her long, elegant fingers.

It didn't help that Khaled was an unkind man, old enough to have grown bitter but still young enough to be callous, as only the young and inexperienced can be.

She yearned for the love her aunties promised would

bud and grow. And, instead, found herself pouring all the love that had been waiting to blossom into Mohammed. For now, she told herself, that was enough.

Morning was Sharifa's favourite time of day, once Khaled had left for his job at the docks and she'd fed and put Mohammed down for his nap. On warm mornings, she'd set his wicker basinet on the old wooden kitchen table next to the window where the sun streamed in through the small, stone courtyard, and on cold, grey days she'd tuck an extra blanket around him and move the table closer to the wood stove and out of the draught. Then she'd start on her work. First, she'd put the dinner on to cook, frying the garlic and onion and ginger in ghee before adding garam masala and chili, then braising the brisket or shin or whatever economy cut was available at the Halaal butcher the day before. She would add two cups of water and bring it to the boil before setting the lid on tight to simmer gently till lunchtime. She would do the rotis in the evening just before they ate; Khaled liked his rotis fresh and she didn't like to make him mad.

Once dinner was on the go, she'd start on the washing and ironing. Sharifa did the laundry for families in the pretty gabled homes that stood side-by-side further down the hill, their neat, white verandas close enough to the sea to offer beautiful views, but far enough away not to smell the stench of the fish market.

She'd wash the soiled linen and grubby clothes in huge steel tubs in the tiny stone courtyard, kneeling down and scrubbing till her knuckles and knees turned raw. After rinsing she'd hang them up, stretching up on tip toes to reach the washing line. How many times had she asked Khaled to lower it for her?

Once they were dry, she'd fill the iron with hot coals from the wood stove, wait for it to heat up, then meticulously iron each piece of laundry, making sure there were perfect lines on every fold of every sheet, and ironing the collars on the men's shirts so stiff they looked starched.

Mohammed would wake up in between and Sharifa would feed and change him and, as he grew a little older, set him down to crawl around at her feet on the stone floor of the kitchen. He would open the kitchen cupboard and pull out the shiny copper pots and lids and play with them until he became bored, then he'd niggle and lift his arms up to her until she picked him up. Most days she'd finish off the dinner with her right hand, with Mohammed on her left hip.

By 4 o'clock every afternoon, Sharifa would drop Mohammed with old Mrs. Lala next door, then trudge down the hill to deliver the tub of fresh laundry to her customers.

If she took a little longer, like on the days when the Cape winds forced her to walk sideways, pressing her small shoulders through it and stopping every few metres to put down the tub and catch her breath, Khaled would already be there by the time she got home. He would rant about having to come home to an empty house and an unfinished dinner, and she would start to say something but hold her tongue. Don't answer back, Auntie Anisa had advised her when, in the early days, she'd complained to her. But he's the one who sent me out to work, he's the one who said we needed the money, she'd protested. Yes, and that makes him feel small. And a small man is a dangerous man. Be patient, my girl, fan his ego, flatter him. This is more for you than for him, please believe me. We are all the sons and daughters of slaves, my child, and some know no other way of being but that one person is owned by another. Auntie Anisa had turned abruptly away and pretended to busy herself with something on the kitchen counter. And Sharifa was starting to understand how secrets begin.

CHAPTER FIFTEEN

2015

HARRY WAS THINKING about secrets on his early morning walk. The ones he'd had, the ones he'd kept for others, the ones which still haunted him all these years later.

He'd been shaken by Calvin's reaction when he'd visited Margot's grave, but not surprised. They'd never addressed the past – how could they when Harry had spent all those years in jail, and Calvin just a child when he went in. Harry had never properly expressed his gratitude to Calvin for working so hard to release him – or his sorrow and regret for what had happened to the family in the aftermath.

When Harry was first released from jail he wasn't talking at all, and when Calvin moved him in to number 17, it took him time to find any words – let alone the words needed to overcome the chasm between them.

They'd picked up their relationship as best they could, but with the shadow of the past sometimes so dark and thick between them it was almost tangible.

Something had to give, and Harry going to the cemetery was that thing. But where to begin?

As it turned out, he didn't have to wait long. Calvin was outside when he turned into the driveway, leaning into the window of a red car parked at the end of it. He stood up and stepped back, and the car started reversing. A dark-haired woman waved at Harry as she reversed past him and out the gate.

Calvin glanced in Harry's direction and turned away, ready to walk to his flatlet at the back of the house.

"Calvin."

Calvin already had his back to him, and lifted his hand to silence him.

"Save it."

"Calvin, please!" Harry's voice was uncharacteristically firm and loud and Calvin stopped walking but didn't turn around.

Harry walked towards him as fast as he could, struggling to gain momentum with his walking stick, and came around to face him.

He paused to catch his breath. "Son, I've wanted to talk to you for so long, but I haven't known where to start."

"You could start with a fuckin' sorry." Calvin's square jaw was set hard. He crossed his arms across his chest and looked down at his father.

"I am sorry, I am so, so sorry, but I…"

"But what? But what?" Calvin's voice was rising.

"Please don't shout, please can we just talk?" Harry pinched the bridge of his nose with his thumb and his forefinger and closed his eyes, suddenly looking older and more tired than he had done in the last five years. "I am trying so hard to see it from your point of view, and honestly it breaks me up when I do. But I wonder if you could stop for a moment to see what it was like for me, to see it through my eyes?"

"See it through your eyes?" his voice was low and angry. "I scheme it wasn't my responsibility to see it through your eyes! Bernice and I was just lighties and Talia was a baby, for fuck's sake! She wasn't even walking yet. But then you wouldn't know that, coz you wasn't there to see her walk or talk or none of that. We needed you, all of us needed you, and you threw us to the wolves!" An image of his stepfather, Kevin, flashed in front of his eyes. "For her! Uncle Clay was more of a father to us than you ever were!"

Harry took a deep breath and slowly let the air out through his mouth. "And don't you think that breaks my heart every single day?" His voice was close to breaking. "Don't you think I regret the way things turned out more than I can ever express in words? That I wanted to be there for you, and Talia and Bernice? And that every moment I've been living here with you these past five years I've been hoping I can somehow make up for all I threw away. You were my life."

"Until we weren't no more." And Calvin's voice was barely a whisper.

Harry paused.

"You are the loves of my life. But so was she. I guess I wanted it all. But, in the end, I lost it all."

"And where did Ma factor into this happy fuckin' little fairy-tale of yours?" Calvin's voice was rising again.

"I know it's hard for you to hear this, Calvin, but your mother and I, our relationship was over a long time ago. If it hadn't been Margot," and he paused, saying her name out loud to him for the first time, "it would have been someone, or something else. I'm not trying to justify what I did, I should have done the honourable thing if I wanted to leave; I should have spoken to her, filed for a divorce and then started a new life. I was a coward in the end and I let everyone down. Please, please forgive me." And now Harry began to cry, tears he thought he'd used up at Margot's graveside but which just kept coming; now that the floodgates were open, they couldn't be closed again.

Calvin looked away, then down at his feet. He shifted uncertainly from one foot to the other. Dropped his hands to his sides then crossed them over his chest again. Then he reached out a hand to Harry and patted him awkwardly on the arm.

"Jah, well what's done is done. There ain't no joling back. We're all just a fucked-up mess and I guess we have to learn to live with it."

Harry dropped his walking stick, then took a tentative step forward. He opened up his arms and put them around his son, and although Calvin didn't hug him back he didn't pull away either and they stood there for a long time, both remembering the last time they'd hugged, more years ago than they cared to count. Harry kneeling in the dusty courtyard of their apartment block, his arms around his little boy. Minutes before the gunshot. Minutes before Margot died.

Holding on to Calvin, his walking stick discarded on the floor, Harry repeated to him what he'd said all those years ago: "I love you, my boy. I love you and your sisters so much."

And this time Calvin, no longer the wide-eyed seven-year-old with the mop of unruly hair and his beloved football at his feet, knew better than to add, "And Ma."

CHAPTER SIXTEEN

1953

NANI SHARIFA SLIPPED easily into the routine of the small household. She would be up every day before dawn and would find Rudo already waiting in the lounge. They would unroll a threadbare prayer rug and sit on their haunches, faces turned towards Mecca. Holding their hands out in supplication, palms facing upwards, they would recite the verses of the Koran separately but together, and afterwards rub their faces with their hands, washing themselves in the words of the prophet. Then they would sit side-by-side in companiable silence and mouth their own private prayers.

Oh Allah, protect my mother, for truly she has made me happy without asking anything in return. Make her happy in this life and in the next. Rudo would pray silently for her mother, as she had done every day when her mother was alive, and continued now that she had gone on to the next life. But a week into their morning prayers together she realised she was praying for Sharifa too. She'd glanced over at her mother-in-law, her small chin raised, her eyes screwed tightly shut and her thin, purple lips moving silently and fervently in prayer, and she'd looked up, imagining her beloved Ali looking down on them and smiling.

After dawn prayers they would go to the kitchen and Rudo would light the wood stove to make tea. She would pour them each a mug of hot, sweet, milky masala tea and they would cup it with both hands, blowing softly at it through clouds of steam. And Leila would find them there, still deep in conversation, when she woke up an hour later to see to the breakfast and get the children ready for school.

The children loved having Nani Sharifa stay, the talcum-scented smell of her, the big, dimpled smile she'd give them – even when they'd been naughty; her cheeks pressed against theirs when she hugged them, warm and soft and squidgy like Ma's bread dough just before it went in the oven.

In the afternoons when they'd come home from school they'd barrel through the front gate, school bags bumping on the ground in a cloud of dust behind them, and see who could be the first to run to Nani. She'd be waiting for them in the high-backed chair she'd carry to the shade of the mango tree at mid-morning each day, and when she spotted them she'd stand up, her arms open wide. She'd have to brace herself from falling as they both flung themselves at her, and she'd be laughing and kissing the top of their warm heads and clucking about their dusty bags all at the same time.

"Nani, Nani, I got a gold star for my stories, look, look!" Harry would shout, pointing to his forehead.

"Nani, I, Nani, I…" Ruby would fumble for something to counteract with.

"You got nothin'! Just tell the truth, Ruby Rhoades!" Harry would say, shoving Ruby on the arm.

"I do too!" Ruby would pout, shoving Harry hard in the chest and sending him reeling.

"Nani, she shoved me!" Harry would start to cry.

"No, I didn't!" Ruby would stand with her arms crossed over her plump chest.

And Nani would soothe them and quieten them down and tell Ruby to apologise to Harry and when Ruby said that he started it, she'd have to tell Harry to apologise to Ruby. By the time they walked in to the house, Nani in the centre with her arms around the two of them, all was forgotten and forgiven. Besides, who could think of anything else once they'd smelt the lunch cooking?

Gogo Rudo would be in the kitchen and they knew better than to be unruly with her, so would each give her a small, tight hug before she bundled them off to wash up, and then the two old women would fuss around the children like a pair of mother hens, making sure they ate all their food and heaping their plates with seconds.

After lunch, Gogo Rudo would instruct them to go for an afternoon nap, and Nani would beckon them with her crooked finger and wrap her arms around them and bend down low and whisper that if they were very good and lay down nice and quietly for their nap, they could look at the magic. And they would both squeal with delight and head off to their room.

There would be some chatter but, soon, their voices would become softer and softer and they'd be asleep.

They'd find Nani outside under the leafy mango tree when they woke up, often having newly washed her hair and sitting out in the sun to let it dry. She wore her hair gathered in a tight little bun at the back of her head, or in a long straight plait down her back, but on days when she washed it, she'd let it hang down by her shoulders – long, thin, grey strands with her white scalp peeking through – and she would comb it over and over until it dried. The children loved to watch Nani comb her hair, and sometimes she'd let them take turns to run the comb through it for her. If they'd fight over who should be first, or who'd had too long a turn, Nani would put her finger to her lips, "shhh" them quietly and gently remind them about their pact. And then they'd try their very best to behave.

Some afternoons Nani would instruct Ruby to pull up a little footstool and sit in front of her while she painstakingly combed the knots out of the little girl's tangled curls, so gently she didn't make a sound – nothing like the crying and screaming that went on when Leila would hurriedly brush it in the mornings before she went to school.

"Nani, why isn't my hair long and soft like yours and Mama's?" Ruby once asked her.

"We all have different hair, my child, and you'll find out, as you grow older, that everyone wants what they don't have," said Nani, kissing her on her crown, turned warm by the sun.

"But I want pretty hair like yours and Mama's!" she pouted.

"Your hair is every bit as pretty as ours, if not prettier – and don't you let anyone tell you otherwise! Look how it curls! Now if only I could make my hair curl like that!"

"You can't?" And Ruby swivelled around on her foot stool to look up at Nani.

"Not a single curl, no!" said Nani, shaking her head. "Just as straight as a pin, as straight as that cockerel's crown," she'd pointed with the comb at the cockerel strutting up and down the dusty yard and Ruby brought her chubby little hands to her mouth and chuckled so hard her shoulders shook.

"A little less laughter from you, miss," Nani smiled, mock smacking her with the tip of the comb, "and a little more sympathy for those of us who don't have your beautiful curls and have to put up with cockerel crowns for hair!"

And Ruby became all puffed up with pride and gave her Nani one of her dimpled smiles.

"I love you, Nani."

"I love you too, my girl."

CHAPTER SEVENTEEN

2015

FOR THE SECOND time in a week, Harry turned into the gate after his morning walk to see Calvin leaning into the window of a red car parked in the driveway.

The woman behind the wheel was reversing past him as he approached the house, and stopped as she came up alongside him.

"Morning, Uncle," she had long, dark hair which she wore loose, and a bright smile. Something about her reminded him of Emma.

"I'm Natalie, Calvin may have mentioned me?"

He didn't have the heart to tell her that Calvin hadn't.

"Oh, yes," he mumbled, "pleased to meet you, Natalie." And he carried on walking towards the house and she continued up the driveway and out the gate.

Calvin was standing at the top of the driveway, examining one of the gutters, rotted through and in no shape for the coming rainy season.

"She seems nice," Harry walked up to him.

"Hmmm?" Calvin looked around, his brow furrowed.

"Natalie, she seems nice."

"Jah." And he turned back to his work.

"Is it serious?"

"Wat?" Calvin looked around again, this time annoyed.

"Is it serious? Seems to me she's a keeper," Harry was resting his hands, one on top of the other, on his walking stick and rocking back and forth on his heels.

"Well now that's rich, relationship advice from my o'man!" He turned back to his work.

"This again?" Harry let out a little sigh. "I thought we were beyond that." And he turned to walk away, his head bent.

"She has a lightie," said Calvin, not turning around.

"What was that?" Harry stopped and looked at him.

"She's got a lightie, a six-year old."

"So?"

"So I don't wanna be no body's baby daddy – and especially if it's some asshole's lightie. That ain't my vibe."

"And what is your vibe, son?" Harry placed his hands on top of his walking stick again.

"To live my life. For me. I don't need no life-long commitments. No fuckin' noose round my neck. What the fuck for?"

"You're a grown man now, son, maybe it's time for a new 'vibe'."

"Jah, well when I want advice from you, I'll aks. Till then, I'll do what I do."

"It would take a braver person than me to try to make you do otherwise," Harry turned away and started slowly walking back towards the house.

Calvin looked over his shoulder at the old man's rounded back, then turned again to inspect the gutters.

Talia gave a low whistle as Calvin walked in.

"Shit, what happened, someone die?" she laughed.

He rolled his eyes at her. "Don't give me your shit."

"Never seen you so dolled up."

"I'm not 'dolled up', what the fuck does that mean anyway?" And he looked up from buttoning his cuffs to glare at her.

Harry stood up from the kitchen table.

"What your sister is trying to tell you is you look good, son."

"Jah, watever. Natalie has some fancy-ass work do, and for some reason wants me to jol. I feel like a fuckin' priest," he said tugging at his shirt collar.

"Jah, like you'd know how that feels!" And Talia laughed raucously.

Calvin rolled his eyes again. "That'll do from the peanut gallery." He walked over to the drinks' cabinet, took out a bottle of Jack Daniels and pulled a silver hip flask from his jacket pocket. He walked back to the kitchen, held the flask over the sink and carefully started filling it.

"What the hell you doing?" asked Talia.

"Ya don't expect me to do this fuckin' freak show sober? Good thing this monkey suit has deep pockets." He closed the lid tight and slipped the flask back into his jacket, patting it with a little smile.

His cell phone started ringing and he pulled it out of his trouser pocket.

"Yo." He was frowning and when he saw Talia and Harry watching him, turned away and walked out the kitchen door.

When he came back he was yanking at his tie, loosening the knot and pulling it down while trying to undo the top button, all at the same time.

"What's going on?" asked Talia.

"We ain't joling. Her loser ex was supposed to have the lightie this weekend, but he's fucked out on her. So it's off, and I can get outta this straight jacket and get into some real clothes and jol to the Club like I wanted to do in the first place."

"Don't be a dick, Cal, tell her to bring her little girl here, we'll babysit; not like I have any plans for the night anyways," said Talia.

"And I'm here too," said Harry, taking a step towards them. "Talia's right, bring her here. We'll babysit and you have your night out. It's for her work."

"I dunno, don't wanna make a habit of it. This is exactly why I don't get involved with chicks with lighties. This is what happens, this is what chicks do!" He stomped his right foot.

"I'm going to break this to you, gently, Cal, she didn't get that lightie alone. There was a dude who played a pretty substantial part in it," said Talia, her elbow propped up on the kitchen counter and resting her chin in her hand.

"Jah, well that dude wasn't me, and that lightie ain't my responsibility – and I was hoping to keep it that way. OK, I'll call her, but I dunno what she'll say. The lightie doesn't know you people."

He walked away again to talk and when he came back, shrugged. "She schemes jah, she'll do it, and schemes thanks. She'll be here in 20 minutes. And I guess I need to get this fuckin' death trap back on," he said, battling again with the top button of his shirt.

"Here, let me help," said Harry. He set down his walking stick and walked over to Calvin who bent down slightly so his father could reach, doing up his top button and tightening the knot on his tie so it fitted snugly in place again.

"Thanks," said Calvin, before turning away and pulling out his phone and scrolling.

Harry looked at his back for a little while, then picked up his walking stick and went into the lounge to sit next to Sabrina. He took her hand and they sat there together watching television.

"Calvin!" A little girl ran into the house and threw herself at him. Harry watched Calvin as he looked down at her, her arms wrapped tight around his waist, and patted her on the head.

"Hey Tam. Wat's happenin' girl?"

She pulled away and grabbed his hand with both of hers, looking up at him, wide-eyed. "Calvin, I got a new doll! Her name's Polly and she's got black hair just like mine and I take her to bed every night with me, and I feed her, well not properly because she's like, a doll, you know, she's not real, but she looks so real, and all my friends at school, they think she's the coolest and they all want to hold her and borrow her for the night, but I say no way, she's my baby and she has to stay with me, they can hold her, right, because mommy says I gotta share, but then when they've held her for a bit too long I get sad and I say Polly needs her dinner now so you'd best give her back, and then I pretend to feed her but like I said she's not a real baby so I don't really feed her, you know? But don't tell the others coz they think she's real!"

Calvin ran two fingers across his lips. "My lips are sealed."

"Sorry, she ran ahead while I was still trying to lock the car," Natalie was standing in the doorway. "Tamara, I told you to wait for me!" And she walked towards her, firmly took her hand and pulled the little girl towards her.

She looked at them apologetically, "She gets really excited, especially when she sees Calvin."

Harry was the first to step forward. "Hello, Tamara, I'm Calvin's dad, it's nice to meet you."

Suddenly shy, she took his extended hand.

"And Natalie, nice to see you again, and may I say you look quite lovely tonight."

She smiled and blushed. He saw Emma again when he looked at her, something in her eyes that was both optimism and sorrow.

"Thank you, Uncle. And thank you so much for offering to babysit Tam tonight. This evening is really important to me."

"It's no trouble at all, we're happy to help," said Harry.

"Oh, and I have something for you," Natalie bent down and took a small casserole dish out of a fabric cooler she'd set down at her feet when she'd arrived. She looked shy as she handed it to Harry. "I'd cooked Tam's favourite dinner for her and her dad tonight, but since he didn't come, I brought it along and thought perhaps you'd like to have it with her."

Harry reached for the dish, closed his eyes and inhaled, a smile on his face.

"Oh my, Natalie! This takes me right back to my Nani Sharifa, the most wonderful woman and possibly the best cook in the world! This smells just like her chicken curry!"

"It's all in the masala – or so my own Nani used to tell me," smiled Natalie, her cheeks growing red as she spoke.

"What's your last name, Natalie?"

"My father is an Ismail."

"The Somerset Ismails?"

"Yes, my father grew up across the road from the Somerset Mosque, on Brooke Street, but then when he and my mom got married they moved to Hillcrest."

"The Moslem or the Christian side of the family?"

"My great grandparents on my mom's side were Moslem, but we were brought up Catholic, like my dad. The other side of the family is still very devout though."

"Hmm," said Harry, setting the casserole dish onto the kitchen counter. "Much like our family: my mother, Leila – Nani Sharifa was her grandmother – was born Moslem but converted and married a Catholic, and that's how we were brought up. I was at school with the Ismails, two brothers, Harold and Anthony."

"Yes, Anthony's my dad."

"A math whizz, I remember that much about him."

"Yup, he had an incredible maths mind but didn't do much with it. When I wanted to go into accounts, he couldn't have been happier," she smiled. "I guess I got to live his dream."

"Do your parents still live there?"

"My dad does, but he and my mom divorced when I was eight and when she remarried and moved to the UK, my older sister and I went with her and did our junior school there. And then when her and my step dad divorced, we came back here, but not to Hillcrest."

"Ah, that's why I can hear a slight accent," said Harry.

"And now that the interrogation is over," said Talia, smiling over at Harry, "I'm Talia."

"Hey, Talia! I think we met once at a braai at Tremayne Harry's house," said Natalie, taking her hand and smiling at her.

Tamara left her mother's side and walked over to Calvin and quietly took his hand.

"Oh jah, I remember, pretty crazy night that! And oh my God, I love your dress!"

"You sure it looks OK?" she asked running her hands down her hips. "It's a little tighter than I'd normally wear – I never really lost the weight after Tam – and a little more sparkly too."

"It's gorgeous. Cal, doesn't she look amazing?"

Natalie smiled at Calvin and adjusted the narrow strap on her right shoulder.

"Ya'll do," the corner of his mouth tightened into a smile and, still holding Tamara's hand, he walked over and put his arm around her waist.

"You don't look too shabby yourself, Calvin Rhoades, you clean up nice," she smiled.

"Jah, well we'd better jol before I change my mind and get outta this fancy dress costume."

"Talia, I seem to remember you saying something about wanting to study accounts when we met that once," said Natalie.

"Oh jah, a bit of a pipe dream, I guess. Much like losing weight," she put her hand on her waist, "I'd really, really like to, but I have no idea when I'd find the time."

"Well, if you're serious I can put you in touch with some people at my firm who qualified through UNISA while working – if you're interested, that is."

"Jah, thanks, I'll give it some thought."

"I think that's a wonderful idea, Tal," said Harry.

"Jah, I said I'd think about it," and Talia turned to the kitchen counter and started stacking dishes.

It was time to go and Natalie knelt down in front of Tamara and brushed her hair out of her eyes with her finger tips. The little girl was all eyes and her bottom lip was starting to quiver.

"Now Tam, you be a good girl, eat your dinner and don't give this nice auntie and uncle any trouble, do you hear me? I've put Polly in your bag, together with a juice bottle, and when you're ready to sleep, your special blanket is in there too. OK, my love? And I won't be long."

Harry stepped forward again.

"Tamara, Sabrina would love to meet you, and she has some dolls too, maybe you can show her Polly and we can introduce you to our doll family?"

The little girl's eyes lit up and she took Harry's hand and let him lead her into the lounge.

Calvin and Natalie took their chance to leave and when Natalie glanced back just before stepping out the door, the little girl was standing with her hands on the arms of Sabrina's wheelchair, peering into her face and smiling as Harry introduced them.

"Come, let's jol," said Calvin, grabbing her hand and pulling her through the door.

CHAPTER EIGHTEEN

1930

THE CANCER MADE an even angrier man of Khaled in death than it did in life. He was so angry with the world around him, Sharifa used to think, that he had no fight left in him for the disease.

Her duty to her husband never wavered and she cared for him and cleaned him and silently withstood his endless criticism and volatile temper. Perhaps it was guilt, she'd think to herself. For not loving him enough. For every other way she'd failed him as a wife.

The night Khaled died, Sharifa was sitting in the upright chair in the corner of his room where she'd taken up nightly residence. It was easier to get to his side when he called from here, easier to avoid his ire when she took too long.

"Sharifa!" she woke up with a start and, still half-asleep, went to the bed. "Sharifa!"

"Yes, I'm here, I'm here," she placed a hand on his feverish arm and he swung his head around, blind in the moment with pain.

"Sharifa." His voice quieter now.

"Yes?"

"I know." He said it so softly she wasn't sure she heard him. She leaned in closer.

"What?"

"I know." He looked at her in the inky light, and there was a moment of clarity when his eyes settled on hers.

"You know what?" Her voice was unsteady. He closed his eyes and she felt him draw in his breath. "You know what, Khaled?" Her voice was rising, panicked, "You know what?"

She started to shake him, gently at first.

"Khaled! Khaled! You know what? Tell me!" She was shaking him harder now, her face close to his, looking deep into his lifeless eyes. "You don't know! You don't know! No one knows!" And her voice broke as she collapsed to her knees next to the bed and buried her head in her hands, her violent sobs shaking her small frame.

By the time she left his room to go next door to inform the neighbours, she had dried the tears. Once the neighbours relayed the message around the community and, within 20 minutes, the men had arrived to prepare his body for burial, the shaking in her hands had stopped. She sat, numb, in the corner of the lounge while the funeral arrangements were made around her, and everyone interpreted her stunned, fixed stare for grief.

Sharifa 1932

I speak to you in my mind all the time, dear Ali, my beloved son. It is all I have now, until the blessed day when we can meet again, In Shaa Allah.

I've imagined the moment I'd see you again so many times. I would take you in my arms and hold you tight, so tight, in fact, that I would never let go. After a long time standing like that, my head against your chest, I would take your hand and lead you to the sofa, the one in the bay window where the sun comes through in sheaths of gold in the late winter afternoons. The sofa where I always sit and think about you, and about our story. I love the beauty of winter afternoons; their magic lies in the fact that they are fleeting, a moment of golden light before the sun sets on the short day. Before the light dies and the cold creeps in. Like so much that we love, it doesn't last.

I would sit down on the right-hand cushion and you would take the left, and I would hold your hand in mine as I talked. I would tell you the whole story as we sat there, side-by-side, till there was nothing more to tell.

But my story may not begin where you'd think, my son. My story would begin with me asking if you remember how the Namaqualand daisies bloom in July, setting the fields on fire; or how, on a clear September morning, Table Mountain seems to rise up from the ocean and tower over our beloved city like a benevolent giant. I would ask if you remember what home feels like. That, I would tell you, my darling Ali, is how love feels too.

CHAPTER NINETEEN

Cape Town 1902

SHARIFA LIKED TO imagine what it was like to live in the houses further down the hill. She never saw much more than the front threshold, as the door was opened just a crack by the servant and held tentatively ajar, then pushed open wide enough to receive the tub she'd hand to them. The door would be hastily closed again, while the clean laundry was unpacked, and re-opened to give back the tub, filled with the next load. At the top would be a small collection of coins.

Sharifa would take the tub and set it down on the front steps, bend down and scoop up the coins and place them in a small drawstring pouch she kept in her pocket, then pick up the tub and head home.

If you asked them, the residents in those pretty little gabled homes would say they weren't wealthy – after all they could only afford one servant, they'd tell you, or they would have been able to do their laundry at home. But Sharifa would walk home dreaming of the life beyond the crack of the door, of the multiple rooms with their high windows and views out on to the sea. On cold days she dreamt of the cosy fireplaces within, marked by the thin trail of smoke from all the chimneys in a row, and saw herself on a plush armchair pulled up close to warm her cold feet. She imagined Mohammed playing on a thick white rug near her, playing with proper toys she'd been able to buy from the general dealers' where she bought her rice and flour. Now that Mohammed was older he recognised toys, and would point at the colourful objects in the window and cry when Sharifa would say no.

Khaled never featured in any of these daydreams, and she'd catch herself and feel guilty.

"Yes?" The door was flung wide open and Sharifa jumped back when she saw a man in the doorway rather than the timid young servant girl who usually greeted her at number 18.

She quickly caught herself and looked down.

"I've brought the laundry," she muttered to the floor.

"Ah," she heard him smile rather than saw it. "Mother said you'd be coming at 4.45, are you always this punctual?" And he reached over and took the tub from her. She handed it to him without looking up. "My golly this is heavy, how do you carry it? It must weigh more than you do!"

She kept staring at her feet.

"Well, thank you for bringing it by," she heard the smile again and saw his feet step back, ready to go inside and close the door again.

"I need the tub," she said so softly he almost didn't hear her.

"What was that?"

She lifted her head slightly but kept her eyes downcast: "I need the tub back. With the dirty laundry."

"Oh, yes, the tub! This is why mother never trusts me with any of her precious household affairs!" And he let out a loud, happy laugh and Sharifa marvelled at the ease and freedom of a laugh like that.

The corner of her mouth tightened into a little smile.

He turned to go back in but left the door open, and now Sharifa raised her head and dared herself to look.

She caught a glimpse of his back, white shirt tucked into brown jodhpurs and long boots. His hair, the colour of beach sand, touched the back of his collar. But she was more interested in what lay beyond – at the size of the hallway, the gas lights already lit though it wasn't yet dark, at the start of a staircase that led upstairs, a richly coloured rug running along the passageway, imitation Persian probably, Sharifa thought, but lovely all the same.

He was back far too quickly and she lowered her eyes guiltily and reached out for the tub.

"There we go," he said, handing it to her. "Are you sure you'll manage?"

"Yes, thank you, I will manage."

As she took the tub from him she searched the top of the pile for the coins but couldn't see any. She began to panic. There was no flour in the house to make the rotis for dinner and Khaled would be mad.

He was getting ready to step inside and close the door again. Sharifa took a step forward and, still looking at the ground, whispered, "I'm sorry, sir, but I think you've forgotten…"

He looked around.

She forced herself to look up at him.

"Excuse me, please, sir, but I think you have forgotten

the money." And she looked quickly down again, but not before seeing that he had unusually green eyes, open and frank like his laugh.

"The money! Of course, the money!" And he slapped his forehead with his open palm. "You must think I'm a total dunce!" Sharifa muttered a protest, but he was already spinning on his heels and rushing back inside.

There was the sound of voices just beyond the threshold and then he was back, holding out a packet which she took from him with a little nod of her head, and turned and started to walk away.

She didn't hear the door shut immediately so waited until she was safely around the corner before she put down the tub and checked that the amount was correct. She emptied the packet into the palm of her hand and the coins jingled as she counted them. There were three extra coins. She turned to go back and tell him that he had made a mistake, that he had paid her too much, but as she approached the house, she saw him step back outside, close the door behind him and head in the opposite direction. She decided she would mention it when she delivered the next batch of laundry. That evening when she picked Mohammed up from Mrs. Lala she had an extra item among her meagre purchases: a little wooden scotch cart with a black horse harnessed to it and real wheels which turned when Mohammed pulled it along the stone floor of the kitchen, squealing with delight at every turn. A gift from Auntie Anisa, she'd lied to Khaled in the evening when he'd asked, irritated by the sound.

For the next week Sharifa scrimped slightly on the size of the rotis – making sure it wasn't enough for Khaled to notice – and made the flour and ghee last longer than usual. And she saved the money to replace the extra she'd been paid.

She had the coins in her pocket when she knocked at the door of number 18 a week later. The young servant answered it as usual.

She reached out to take the tub from her and Sharifa passed it to her. When she came back with the dirty laundry and that week's payment, Sharifa said, softly: "The master, who was here last week, I think he made a mistake with the money."

"Master's gone. I don't know anything about money. If it was short you must take it up with the madam, but she is resting now and does not want to be disturbed."

"It wasn't short," but she had already retreated inside and shut the door.

He wasn't there the next week or the week after that and Sharifa, rather than try again to explain her predicament, hid the money away in her clothes drawer, reluctant to spend it before he returned.

She'd almost forgotten about it when she knocked on the door at number 18 almost two months later and it was flung open. Before she could drop her gaze, she found herself looking up into a pair of green eyes.

"Ah, still as punctual as ever, I see!" And he laughed good naturedly. "Here, let me take that from you."

"Thank you," she mumbled, looking down at the floor.

She waited for him to step inside and looked quickly to see if anything had changed since last time.

He was back all too soon, the coins on the top as usual.

"See, you can teach an old dog new tricks!"

"Sir?" She glanced up at him and then down again.

"I said you can teach an old dog new tricks, I remembered the tub and the money this time!"

"Yes, sir, but last time you overpaid me. I had been keeping the money for you but then you went away." She said it all in a rush.

"There was no overpayment, I don't know what you're talking about." She looked tentatively up and he winked, and she quickly looked away again.

Then she mumbled a breathless thank you and almost ran down the steps.

Again, the door didn't close immediately, and she didn't count the coins until she was around the corner. And, again, there was more than usual. She couldn't help but smile, pushing down the irrational guilt which surfaced again that evening when she added the extra money to the little stash in her drawer.

"Do you like to read?" he said the next week as he flung open the door and reached hurriedly for the tub.

"Sir?"

"Do you like to read?"

"I do not know how to read well." She didn't take her eyes off the floor. "My little boy, Mohammed, loves books, though he can't yet read. I would like him to read better than me."

"Splendid. Wait here."

This time there were no extra coins, but a bundle of books on top of the laundry.

"Books give wings to the mind and flight to the imagination," he said as she took the tub from him.

"Sir?" she glanced up.

"Plato. And I know books have often helped me fly far away from places," he looked back at the house behind him with a sad smile. "Books show us a world of possibilities we never even knew existed. I hope your son enjoys them."

She tightened the corner of her mouth in a smile, and rushed down the stairs.

The next week the door was flung open just as she lifted her hand to knock. He was dressed in a jacket and hat, a walking stick in his hand, and they almost collided on the steps.

"Steady on," he laughed, grabbing the tub from her before she dropped it. "I'll just swap out the laundry and then I can walk with you, I'm on my way out."

She protested but he didn't pay any attention, running inside and returning moments later with the dirty laundry. She reached for it but he held on to it.

"I'll carry it for you as long as we're going in the same direction, then you can take over."

Her cheeks were burning, imagining what people would think seeing her walking down the road with this White man, but it would have been more difficult to explain to him why she shouldn't than to just go along. He was talking but her mind was so muddled she wasn't listening. Then she heard Mohammed's name and started to pay attention.

"Did he like the books…your little boy…Mohammed, is it?" He looked over at her but she didn't meet his gaze.

"Yes, sir, thank you, he enjoyed them very much. Thank you."

"Please, it's Evan, not sir! Sir is my father – or my father's father. I'm just Evan."

"I can not call you that." She said it quietly but firmly.

"You can't?" And then he laughed, but there was none of his usual joy in it, and added, "Of course you can't. Forgive my insolence. I'm not good at convention, maybe you noticed?"

She didn't answer and they walked along in silence for the next block, Sharifa slowing her pace to fall a couple of steps behind him.

"Well, this is where we part ways," he said, stopping and turning to her, handing her the tub. She took it from him and he tipped his hat slightly and made to walk away.

"Sharifa," she said, so softly he almost missed it.

He turned to look at her, smiled and said, very softly too, "Good bye, Sharifa."

CHAPTER TWENTY

1954

TWO MONTHS IN Bulawayo led to three and then four, and Sharifa knew she would have to leave eventually and go back to Cape Town, but two things were preventing her. How attached she'd become to the family, especially her darling Harry and Ruby, and how to find the courage to do what she had come here for.

Sharifa felt most at peace during those quiet mornings after dawn prayers, sitting beside Rudo, the guiding hand of Allah on her shoulder, supporting her and giving her strength.

Often in those quiet moments she thought she may find the strength to begin. And then her courage would fail her and she'd grow silent again.

She sometimes wondered why, after all these years and after all they had been through, it was so important for her to talk about it. But Sharifa sensed in her increasing breathlessness that she didn't have much longer on this earthly plane, that soon she would be facing her creator. And she wanted to face Him free of the burden of the past, unbridled by the secrets and the shame that had shadowed her.

She also felt she owed it to Ali, and, in his stead, his beloved Rudo. The time for pretence, for hiding, was over. If they loved her as she loved them, they would not cast her away. And yet the nagging voice of doubt still plagued her and turned her courage into fear.

Then one day in mid-winter, the darkness of the cold morning still so dense they could sense but not see each other sitting close together on the prayer mat, Rudo provided an opening.

They'd finished their private prayers and were sitting in comfortable silence as they did every morning, each lost in their own thoughts.

"What was Ali's father like?" She had never asked about him before.

Sharifa felt her heart in her throat. She took a deep breath. "He was a complicated man." Rudo sensed the sadness in her voice and although she knew she should leave it at that, she also felt compelled to know more of the man who had formed the one half of her beloved Ali.

"He had demons?"

"We all have demons, my dear child. Some of us are just better at hiding them." Her voice grew quiet. "My darling Ali had his own, though he hid them by filling his life with joy, with laughter," she paused and turned to Rudo in the darkness, "with love."

"Ma, how much of our past do you think colours our future?" Rudo asked.

"All of it, my girl, in one way or another. All our sorrows and all our guilt, as well as all our joy and happiness are the threads of the tapestry that form our lives. But it's up to us what tapestry we choose to hold up to the world. Do we use the pain to cause pain in others, or do we try to turn the sorrow into joy? We all deal with it differently. Ali showed only love and joy to the world, despite any pain he may have felt."

"As did you." The women were sitting so close, Sharifa could feel Rudo's words hang in the air like the mist of her breath. She took a sharp breath. Rudo reached in the darkness for her small, bony hand and held it in her own, gently stroking it with the other. "You never talk about it, but I sense it sometimes, in your expression when you don't know anyone is watching, the way you hold the children so tight. I know you carry so much pain, Ma, and I need you to know that you can always count on me. That you can always talk to me. That I have come to love you like my own dear mother, may Allah rest her soul."

Rudo heard a sob catch in Sharifa's throat.

"Don't hold it in, it's OK. It's OK to cry."

And then she leaned forward and took the old woman in her arms, feeling her sharp shoulders through her kameez, and she held her and stroked her hair, like Auntie Yasmin had stroked Sharifa's hair all those years ago when she'd gone over to her house with a broken lip; and Sharifa finally let go, allowing herself to feel it all, the sorrow, the fear, the guilt, the pain. Like a mud dam breaking under the strain of a mighty river, the tears came, flooding her. But she realised in that moment that they wouldn't drown her as she had always feared they would. She was safe.

From that day onwards, the two women's morning routine changed a little. They still met before dawn in the lounge, they still sat side-by-side as they prayed separately, together. They still had their time for private meditation and prayer. But then Rudo would shuffle a little closer to Sharifa, their knees touching and their hands clasped together, and Sharifa would tell her the story of her life, very slowly, just a little at a time; the time passed so quickly before the rest of the household would be awake, and the pain of the past, like a bitter medicine, could only be taken in small doses.

CHAPTER TWENTY-ONE

Cape Town 1902

THE WINTER MONTHS were the hardest. If it wasn't the wind, it was the driving rain. Sometimes it was both at the same time. By the time Sharifa reached number 18, or any of the other households she worked for, she was often shivering with cold.

It was a day like that, mid-July, when she knocked on the door and it was opened by a man who looked so much like Evan and, yet, so disconcertingly different that when she glanced up, she gasped.

He had dark hair and olive skin but the same striking green eyes – though a hardness in them that made him look cruel. There was a rigidity in his mouth too, and his square jaw, so beguiling on Evan, was stubborn and unyielding on this face.

"Yes!" It was a command rather than a question.

"I have come with the laundry." Sharifa made to hand it to him but he stepped back inside and closed the door without taking it. Exhausted, she set it down on the steps and waited, and heard him just inside the doorway tell someone that the 'coolie washer woman' was outside.

The servant girl silently appeared and took the laundry, bringing it back loaded up with dirty laundry and the usual collection of coins on the top.

She took the tub and headed back down the street and couldn't shake the strange uneasiness in her.

Evan called her name but she was so lost in thought she didn't hear him.

He came up to her, out of breath, and smiling. "I missed you when you came to the house. I had these for you." And he held out a small pile of slim books. "I've been helping out in adult literacy classes, I hope you don't think me presumptuous, but I thought, maybe, and only if it's something you would like to do" – he stammered – "you may like to improve your reading with these."

She put the tub down on the pavement in front of her and took the books, her head still bent.

"Thank you." Her voice was small.

"It's nothing." And for the first time since she'd met him, he looked down and stared at his feet. "Well, I guess I'd better be going. My big brother, Thomas, is here from the Transvaal and has wild plans to train me up into the family business and make a gentleman of me." She glanced up and he rolled his eyes. "All I can say is I wish him luck in that!" And he laughed cheerfully.

With that he nodded in her direction and ran back down the hill.

Sharifa put the books on top of the laundry and carried on walking, unreasonably excited as she passed signs in shop windows that she saw every day and longed to be able to read.

Despite the cold and the wind, she quickened her step and headed home.

CHAPTER TWENTY-TWO

Sharifa 1932

IF YOU UNDERSTAND love, my darling Ali, which I think, after loving Rudo as you have, you do, you may understand a little better what I must tell you next. I have been afraid and cowardly – and I still am. But I realise this secret and this story do not belong to me alone. It is your secret and your story too.

You may remember, when you were a child, that I was not able to write much more than my name. I did not go to school, my dear son, and this is why it was so important for me to see you well educated, to see that you and Mohammed could read. It was one of the few things your father and I agreed on. That you should read and write well. His views about me doing so were not the same. I learnt to write when he wasn't watching, and this, my Ali, became the first of many secrets. The problem with secrets is that soon they are followed by more. They pile up, one upon the other, until they hide the truth altogether. It's a dangerous road and once you are on it, you are sure to crash.

You may even remember the crash, when it came. You were a little boy, five years old maybe. You may have a recollection of shouting and screaming. You may remember my swollen lip the next day. You may have seen the words carefully written on sheets of manila paper torn up and thrown into the flames, scattered like moths attracted fatally to the light. I had written your names on the page over and over again. Ali and Mohammed. Ali and Mohammed. I wanted to make them perfect. Perfect like you. I watched your names go up in flames. First the edges, blackened and curling, the fire licking and tasting it until, in a sudden burst, they were caught up. Ignited. Consumed. And the fire that burnt them was still not as intense as the white-hot pain that raged through me.

So this, my Ali, is the first of my confessions. I had learnt to write your names.

Of course, your father didn't hit me because I was learning to read and write. He hit me because of what it meant, because he knew that once I could write, I could pen him out of my life. I could write my own future. A small man is an angry man. My Auntie's words come back to me all the time. A husband who could not read would never tolerate a wife who could. Nor would he tolerate all the other pursuits which would be sure to follow.

My darling Ali, he was right about one thing. I was guilty. And I deserved to be punished.

"Why don't you come to the classes?" Evan asked as he walked Sharifa down the road. It was becoming a regular occurrence and she'd stopped protesting. It was never more than a block or two, then he would veer off towards the city and she would head back up the hill. And she welcomed the help with the heavy tub – and the company.

"I can not."

"It's one hour a week, that's all. It's quite safe, you know."

"I'm not afraid." And she wasn't afraid of the classes.

"Then what?"

"It is difficult."

"Yes, of course. Well, think about it. It's in the Catholic church hall. Every Tuesday from 2 to 3. This is me!" And he handed her the tub before cheerfully tipping his hat and heading up the street.

Half-way through that first day in class, my darling Ali, as Allah is my witness, I nearly got up and left! The people were friendly enough, but I was the only woman there with her head covered, the only Moslem woman in the room. I felt so out of place. I felt I did not belong there. I had left Mohammed with Mrs. Lala and told her I had extra laundry deliveries. I had even carried the tub all the way to class, full of our own clothing, to cover up my lie. That was another cause for my awkwardness. I was the only person in the room with a laundry tub by her desk!

The desks were very small, I think they use them for the Catholic children's Madressa, but as I am so small I fitted my knees under it well. There were some men there too, huge Black men with clean-shaven faces, and bearded Afrikaner men in veldskoene and shorts, showing their ruddy knees and squeezed untidily into the little desks. I had never seen people of all races and ages, men and women, sitting together in one room like that. I was about to get up and leave and then I noticed that everyone felt as out of place as I did. Everyone was a little nervous to be there, for different reasons. I stayed for that, but I also stayed because it would have been more embarrassing to get up in the middle of class and walk out of class carrying a giant tub of laundry!

The priest instructing them was a tall, thin man with short, red hair, parted at the side and Bryl-creamed flat. Sharifa, head tilted down but looking shyly up, imagined he was one of those people whose hair, if they left it to grow, would be wild and unruly. She wondered if his long, stiff black robe had the same effect on his body.

"Why are you here?" He was addressing the entire room and she liked the lilt in his voice. "Go on, tell me, what made you come? Don't be shy."

A small-built man with a closely shaven head put up his hand.

"Yes, son?" the priest nodded in his direction.

"I want to get a better job," he said in a small voice.

"Good, good. Anyone else?" the priest spread his arms to encourage more responses.

"I want to read to my children." It was a woman sitting in the front row.

"Excellent. Anyone?"

When no one else spoke, he continued. "You have all taken a very brave step coming here today, and I salute you. Whatever your circumstances, your race, your religion, you have come here to better yourself, to better your families, and there is surely, in the eyes of God, nothing more honourable than that."

Sharifa looked down and smiled to herself, happy to think her coming here may be seen by Allah as an honourable act.

"OK, then let us begin."

Evan stood to the side of him, chalk poised in front of a giant blackboard.

"Evan has written out the alphabet for us, let us begin, together, to recite it."

And as Evan pointed to each letter, the priest read the alphabet, the class repeating after him.

"A is for apple, B is for ball, C is for cat…."

Sharifa was mumbling the words under her breath, afraid to speak too loudly in case she was saying it wrong.

"Z is for zebra, and that is the end of the alphabet. Thank you, Evan. Now Evan will hand out a pencil and a piece of paper to each person."

When he came alongside her desk Evan was beaming. "You came," he whispered, and she glanced up quickly, taking the pencil and paper from him.

Then she spent a difficult hour trying to train her fingers to hold the pencil correctly and reproduce the cursive letters Evan had written on the board.

Evan and the priest walked around the room, checking on progress and helping where it was needed. "May I?" Hearing the priest's voice beside her, Sharifa looked up and nodded. He rested his left hand on the back of her chair and used his right hand to gently guide her hand over the paper.

The letters began to magically appear and Sharifa could feel the excitement in her chest.

She was so excited after that first lesson she practically ran home. She first ran to the bedroom and hid the pencil and sheafs of paper, then went next door to collect Mohammed.

"Your cheeks are bright," said Mrs. Lala, examining her closely when she opened the door.

"Mama!" Mohammed squealed when he heard the door open and ran to his mother, and Sharifa used the diversion to avoid replying.

She went down on her haunches and hugged him, buried her head in his sweet-smelling hair.

"My Mohammed."

When she stood back up, Mohammed's little hand in hers, Mrs. Lala was still watching her closely.

"Thank you for having him, see you tomorrow," and she quickly turned and left, squeezing Mohammed's hand tight.

"Did Salmaan read your book to you today, my boy?" Salmaan, Mrs. Lala's 12-year old grandson, spent most afternoons at the house.

"Yes, mama!" And he looked up excitedly at her. "The old man who lived on the hill was friends with all the forest animals."

"Really? And what kind of animals were there?"

"There was a yabbit, a bear, some singing birds, all the forest animals, Mama."

And Sharifa smiled as he retold the tale, squeezing his hand a little more.

"Where did Mohammed's reading books come from?" Khaled was sitting in front of the fire, his body blocking out all the heat. He kept his eyes fixed on the flames as he spoke.

"One of my customers gave them to me," said Sharifa,

busying herself with washing the dinner dishes.

"Which one?"

"Mrs. Godwin." Sharifa kept her voice steady.

"Where does she live?" he glanced back at her now.

"Number 18. You know Mrs. Godwin, she was one of my first customers."

He didn't reply but went back to staring at the fire. And Sharifa could feel her cheeks grow hot.

Sharifa 1954

"I've let so many people I love slip through my fingers, my dear Rudo. Mohammed and Ali – they left when they were so young, when their lives had just begun – you and dear Leila, and others…" her voice trailed off.

"I wonder, sometimes, how much I changed from the young girl I was, how much I was changed by the people I loved and lost, the things I followed – and those I did not.

"There was something about going to those classes which made me feel so strong – maybe for the first time in my life. Strong, and able to decide my own destiny. I was a simple girl, from a simple family. I didn't have big dreams, my dear child. I thought, growing up, that all I wanted was a good husband, a comfortable home and children, that I would leave all the rest to the men in my life. But then my father died and my husband had a heart too hard or too closed, I guess I'll never know which, to care. I found myself alone.

"Time and years changed me. I imagined my life in that one house, with that one narrow view, and I wanted more. You know, I never really knew that, or perhaps never really admitted that, till I sat behind a tiny child's desk in a church room, and heard the alphabet being spoken out loud. Oh, the possibilities that suddenly flashed before my eyes, I could hardly contain my excitement.

"Had I known then where that excitement would lead me, would I have stopped? Would I have exchanged my new-found glimpse of freedom for what would follow? I can not answer that, my dear Rudo; but knowing what I know now, that any path different to the one I took may have meant not having my beloved Ali, or not being able to read and write and encourage others to do the same, I would do it all over again. Because people may come and go, wealth may come and go, our health is the same. But what I learnt in those classes, no one could take away from me."

CHAPTER TWENTY-THREE

2015

"YOU EMBARRASSED ME!" Natalie's voice was tight with emotion.

"Why? Because I don't twang like your fancy friends – like you when you're with them!" Calvin's voice turned falsetto: My name is Natalie and my, my I am so pleased to meet you, please forgive my boyfriend, he's so raw, but what can I say, he's a good fuck!"

"You are an asshole." She said it quietly. Her hands, gripping her car keys, were trembling.

"Jah, I am. What I've been tunin' you all along. I'm an asshole, a waste of fuckin' time who'll never amount to nothin'. I been telling ya, but ya don't wanna listen, coz you scheme ya can change me, scheme ya can take me outta the ghetto. Make a man of me!" And he snorted. "A fancy man who dresses in fuckin' penguin suits and twangs and sips on red wine!" He tugged at his tie and threw it on the ground. "Well, Nat, it ain't gonna happen. This is who I am and I ain't never gonna change, not for you, not for nobody, not for nothin'! Not to be your fancy man, not to be your baby daddy! I never aksed for none of that. This is fuckin' me!"

And he beat both hands on his chest. "We ain't right for each other – what I been telling you all along. You can do better than me – you can get anyone you smaak, don't know why you have to pick on me. You could have your boss – he'd do you!" he turned and pointed at her. "Maybe he already is, I dunno, but scheme the way he looks at you, he's into more than your accounting skills. So after tonight, maybe ya'll get the message and stop running after me."

"Running after you?" And her voice was small and unsteady.

"Ya heard me." He turned to the kitchen counter and with one hand resting on it, used the other to take out the hip flask from his pocket. He flicked off the lid with his thumb, tossed back his head and lifted it to his lips.

Natalie watched him for a few moments, turned to walk away, then walked back and spoke to his back. "You didn't embarrass me because of the way you talk, or what work you do, or what you think you are. You embarrassed me because you were rude and disrespectful to me. You embarrassed me because you acted like you didn't want to be there with me at all, and, until now, I thought that was just an unreasonable feeling. Thank you, Calvin. Thank you for confirming it."

Talia and Harry were in the lounge with Tamara asleep on the couch between them.

When Natalie hurried in from the kitchen and saw them sitting there, she started to frantically brush the tears from her eyes.

"I'm so sorry for keeping you up so late," she said, visibly trying to pull herself together. "Thank you for looking after Tam, I hope she wasn't any trouble." Her trembling voice belied her bright, fixed smile.

She was packing away Tamara's things as she walked towards them, shoving them into the bag as quickly as possible.

Talia jumped up and started helping her.

"It was no trouble at all," she said.

"We loved having her, and so did Sabrina," added Harry. "And your curry was every bit as delicious as it smelt, it reminded me so much of my beloved Nani, you have no idea." Harry shook his head lightly.

Natalie smiled shyly. "Thank you, thank you again." And her voice was quivering.

She went over to the couch to lift Tamara, and Talia turned and started to call Calvin to come and help.

"No, please," said Natalie, half turning to her but not meeting her eyes, "I'll do it."

Talia carried Tamara's bag and blanket while Natalie leant down and picked the little girl up.

She squirmed in her arms and Natalie whispered softly to her that it was OK, that mommy was here, that she could go back to sleep, and she kept talking soothingly to her as she walked out the door and towards the car.

Talia ran up ahead and opened the back door for Natalie, and when she lay the little girl on the seat and straightened up, she handed her the bag and blanket.

Natalie took them from her, laying the blanket over Tamara and placing her bag on the car floor in front of her.

She said a hurried thank you and goodbye, got into the car and started up the engine. Harry, in the meantime, had taken a slow walk to the gate and when she reversed up the drive-way he opened it for her. She waved to him through the closed window and he could see that she was crying. By the time he closed the gate and walked back towards the house, he could hear Talia's raised voice.

Calvin was still standing with one hand on the counter, drinking from the hip flask.

"What the fuck is wrong with you? Why do you have to turn everything to crap? Why, Calvin? Why?"

Harry walked in and placed a hand on Talia's arm.

"No, Dad, he has to hear this! He can't just keep fuckin' his way through every woman in this town, and hurting people who genuinely care about him."

Calvin tipped his head right back and drained the last drop. Without saying a word he walked around to the drinks' cabinet, took the still half-full bottle of Jack Daniels out and, gripping it by the neck, walked out of the house and up the driveway.

They heard the gate screech open and bang shut and they looked at each other but neither spoke.

CHAPTER TWENTY-FOUR

Cape Town 1902

"HOW DID YOU like the class?" Evan was walking her down the street, carrying the laundry tub.

"It was difficult, but I liked it."

"It will be difficult at first, but don't give up."

"I won't give up."

And he looked over at her, surprised by the tone in her voice. Then he smiled. "I shouldn't imagine you give up on anything."

"What do you mean?"

"You're a strong woman, Sharifa, that much is obvious. And I don't think it's been easy for you. You never give up." His voice was sombre.

She didn't reply, and after walking a few steps in silence, he started laughing at a cartoon from the Cape Argus tied on to the trunk of a tree – "Those crazy Afrikaners are at it again" – and the moment passed.

But Sharifa walked the rest of the way home that day with his words ringing in her head. "You never give up." And she couldn't seem to separate the twin feelings of thrill and fear that coursed through her.

Sharifa had started looking forward to her time with Evan, walking a couple of blocks down the street once or twice a week. In those moments she felt like a completely different person: free, unfettered, not a mother, not a Moslem wife, just Sharifa. Evan would do most of the talking, Sharifa still walking a step or two behind him for propriety. He spoke about their farms in the Transvaal, how he loved the contrast to Cape Town but missed the sea, "every single day I am away from it."

He spoke a little about his family, about how when his father died, his older brother, Thomas, took charge of the home and the businesses and how he had tried to convince Evan to become more interested in them too.

"It doesn't make me happy. I'm not Thomas. He can make the money and have it, for all I care!" he'd laughed.

He spoke to her about education, about how reading and writing when he was a little older would open up Mohammed's opportunities to the world, help him decide his own destiny. And hers too. He glanced over at her and although she didn't meet his eyes, she'd felt her heart beat faster.

He still helped with the literacy classes when he was in town, and although he would always smile warmly when he saw her there, curled up at her little desk, her head down, they never talked. But sometimes, as they walked, she would ask him a question that had been troubling her from class.

"What is the difference between t-h-e-i-r and t-h-e-r-e? Father Patrick explained it in class, but I still don't understand. And sometimes I find it hard to understand his accent."

And he'd spend five minutes, gently and patiently explaining and she would instantly understand, nodding her head excitedly and, when she got home, scribbling it on her sheaf of paper before tucking it away again in the drawer.

It was spring in Cape Town. Sharifa remembered that clearly because the jacarandas had started to bloom, settling like purple frost on the tips of the trees and laying down a plush carpet under their feet, buds popping softly as they trampled them.

It was about six months into her lessons and she hadn't seen Evan for a few weeks. She was lost in thought and wasn't expecting him to open the door that day.

When she glanced up at him, she knew instantly that there was something wrong.

"Hello, Sharifa. Let me get the laundry sorted and then walk with you." His voice was flat.

He came out and although his eyes were hooded by his hat, she could sense a heaviness in them. They walked a block without saying a word.

"You've been away on the farms?" she asked as a way of breaking the uncharacteristic silence between them.

"Yes, I have."

"Father Patrick has missed you in class." There was so much left unsaid in that one sentence.

Evan looked over at her and smiled sadly.

"Sharifa, I'm going to be going away again, and I'll probably be gone a long time." She'd never heard him sound so sad.

"Where are you going?" What was this leaden panic that had settled suddenly in her chest?

"My family – well, Thomas – wants me to fully take over the running of our farms in the Transvaal. They think it's time I took more interest in the family business. They think it's time I took on more responsibilities."

"Is that what you want?"

"You know what I want." And she felt her cheeks grow hot. The unexpected ache in her chest was so great she thought she may not be able to breathe.

"But you are a wonderful teacher. You should talk to your family."

"There's no point. My destiny was decided for me long before I was born."

She glanced over at him.

"So, when you spoke about reading and writing, about it giving us the power to decide our own future, what did you mean?" said Sharifa in a quiet voice. She had stopped walking but continued to look down at the ground as she spoke.

"I guess I was wrong." He was looking straight ahead.

"Why would you open the door to possibilities, then close it again?" The dual meaning hung heavily in the air.

"Sharifa." He had also stopped walking. He put down the tub and turned to her, but she wouldn't meet his gaze. "I have no choice. It is decided. I leave on Monday."

He thrust his hands in his trouser pockets and started to dig in the sand with the toe of his shoe, staring at the ground.

She took a deep breath. "Class will not be the same without you," she said quietly. She turned to him, still not looking up, bent down and lifted the tub.

"Sharifa…"

She looked up and smiled, but could feel the tears pricking at her eyes and couldn't let him see her cry.

"I am grateful for all you have done for me, for your kindness," she said in a quiet voice. He tried to speak but she silenced him with a little shake of her head. "I can never repay you for encouraging me to learn, it has meant more to me than you know. Thank you, Evan." She paused, saying his name for the first time and looking him straight in the eye. "I wish you luck – and happiness." Her voice was small and tight. Then she turned away and headed quickly down the hill, her eyes blinded by tears.

CHAPTER TWENTY-FIVE

2015

CALVIN DIDN'T COME home that night, which wasn't unheard of. But when he didn't come home for two more nights, Talia and Harry began to become concerned.

"Have you checked with your mother?" Harry asked Talia on the morning of the third day. He was sitting across from Sabrina and wiping porridge from around her mouth with a wet face towel, before lifting each of her little hands in turn and gently cleaning them.

"Ma says she hasn't seen or heard from him – neither has Bernice," said Talia, hopping from one foot to the other as she slipped on her pumps with one hand, holding a piece of toast in the other. "I don't have time for this, he's a grown-ass man and can look after himself." But there was no hiding the concern in her voice.

"I suppose there's no point checking with Natalie?" Harry was drying Sabrina's hands with a towel.

"She'd be an idiot to take him in, I'd like to think she's smarter than that."

"We're not always so smart when it comes to love," said

Harry, looking up and smiling out of the corner of his mouth.

"Jah, well, as I said, I'm not babying him, I have enough on my plate and, anyway, I'm late for work."

"Have you given any more thought to what Natalie said about UNISA?"

"To be honest, Dad, I haven't had time."

"Make time, my girl, this is your future – and Sabrina's."

She didn't reply but came over to them, the half-eaten toast still in her hand, bent down and kissed Sabrina on the forehead and whispered, "Bye bye, baby girl. Be good for grandpa and see you when I get home."

Then she pecked Harry on the cheek and started to walk towards the door.

"Make sure to eat that toast, I didn't make it for decoration," Harry called after her, and, not looking around, she lifted her free hand and waved to him.

When Clayton visited later that day, Harry expressed his concerns about Calvin.

"You know how self-destructive he can be," said Harry, sitting on a chair under the overhang of the veranda, one hand on Sabrina's as she sat beside him in her wheelchair. Clayton was perched on the low wall that ran along it. "Sometimes I see so much of Gwennie's recklessness in him."

"I don't think Gwennie is the only reckless one in this family," Clayton said, smiling kindly at him.

Harry sighed and looked down at the ground. "You're right, my old friend, Calvin got lumped with two parents who act first and think later."

"Now don't be too hard on yourself, in all fairness you

were only reckless when it came to Margot," Clayton leaned forward slightly, his two bony hands resting on his thin knees."

"Well you see that's the thing, I think this new woman of his, Natalie's her name, really means a lot to Calvin; I honestly think he's smitten, and that's scaring him half to death. So he's doing what Calvin always does when he's scared: he's running."

"Natalie? Natalie who?"

"Natalie Ismail – the Somerset Ismails. You must remember them, two brothers, Anthony and Harold. We were at school with Anthony – he was always top of the class in maths. His daughter, Natalie, she's taken after him, she's been to college and qualified as an accountant, works for some fancy firm. She's going places, that girl."

"And she's hooked up with Calvin." said Clayton with a furrowed brow. "He can be quite the charmer, our boy, Calvin, and if this Natalie is smart like you say, she'll have seen through the macho act and figured out he's pretty damn smart too. And smart or not, girls go potty for his looks," and Clayton shot him a sideways look, "much like they did for another Rhoades man I could mention! You old dog!" He gave a short laugh. "Boy, did it used to get my goat, how the girls would all go ga-ga over you. And there was me, with my croos hair and my skinny legs! Luckily your sister liked skinny legs!"

Harry laughed. "Would you believe me if I told you I didn't even notice? Honest to God I did not know they were looking at me!"

"Oh, I believe you alright!" Clayton nodded. "I've never met anyone more clueless about women or unconcerned about their appearance as you were. For a while there you were so oblivious to women I began to think maybe you batted for the other side, if you know what I mean?" And Clayton winked at him.

"What, you thought I was gay?" and he quickly raised a hand defensively. "Not that I'm saying there's anything wrong with that; I've come a long way since we were all young and stupid and what-not, but, no, I always liked women, I just didn't know what to do about it – about them."

"And that's where you and Calvin are different – streets apart, in fact. Calvin knows how good looking he is and he uses every bit of it to his advantage. You dealt with your fear of women by ignoring them, Calvin deals with his by losing himself in them – the more the better, but only a moment at a time. So when one comes along and it looks like she may stick – when he secretly hopes she will but doesn't know how to deal with it, questions if he's good enough, if he deserves her – well that's when he runs. And that boy is gonna keep on running all his life if he doesn't wake up."

"Gwennie sorted me out in that department," said Harry, looking down.

"Gwennie knew a good thing when she saw it," nodded Clayton.

"Though I don't regret any of it – how can I when I look at the kids?" And he squeezed Sabrina's hand.

"Of course you don't! Our lives take a course and without us being able to see what lies ahead, we do the best we can with what little knowledge we have." Then he looked up, his suddenly cheery voice cutting into the sombre mood. "Hey, you ever think about dating again? Here we are worrying about Calvin's love life, but you still have some life left in you, you old codger, what are we going to do about you? Don't you think it's about time you got back in the saddle?" He slapped Harry playfully on the arm.

"What? Now I'm really sure you've gone and lost your marbles! Me date? Are you serious? I know about as much about dating as I know about using a computer, and I can tell you for free I don't even know how to turn one on!"

"Are we talking about a computer or a woman now?" said Clayton, throwing his head back and slapping his thighs as he laughed at his own joke.

"Very funny," laughed Harry. "Hell, I'd sooner go back in time and take on dinosaurs than go back into the world of dating and women!"

"Ah, methinks you protest too much, my friend," laughed Clayton. "I think you've still got some fire in those old bones, I'd wager you could still turn a head or two." He winked again at Harry and the two talked and laughed until it was time to take Sabrina in to get ready for dinner and for Clayton to head home to Ruby.

Harry watched his old friend reverse out of the gate and disappear down the road.

"Dating! Huh! I've never heard anything more ridiculous in my life," he muttered softly to himself, shaking his head. But as he walked back down the driveway to the house, he couldn't help smiling.

Calvin was home by the fourth day. Harry and Talia had no idea how he got home, or when, but that morning when they came into the kitchen to get breakfast ready, he was there, boiling the kettle for his morning coffee. His jowls were dark with stubble and his soft curls were tousled and standing up on end.

"Well look what the cat dragged in," said Talia with a sideways glance before pushing past him to get to the stove.

"Morning, son," said Harry. "We've been worried about you." Calvin grunted. He poured boiling water over the coffee granules in his mug, took a sip, squinting through the steam, then walked out the door.

"Well good morning to you too," said Talia to his back before reaching for the kettle and pouring some of the boiled water into a pot to mix with oats for Sabrina's breakfast.

Neither of them saw Calvin for the rest of the day, but when he came through in the evening to rummage in the fridge for dinner, he was looking much more rested and had combed his hair and shaved.

He still didn't say a word to them, but when he'd dished up a plate of leftover roast chicken, heated it in the microwave and was getting ready to go eat it in his apartment, he paused and walked over to Sabrina.

"What's happenin', girl?" he said in the soft voice he reserved for his niece. "These clowns been treating you right? Nah? Well, me neither," and he smiled at her out the corner of his mouth and bent down and kissed her on the cheek before turning around and leaving.

Calvin was working at the deceased artist's house again, and was gone most of the day, coming wordlessly into the house each evening to look for dinner which he'd take and eat alone in his apartment. About a week after his disappearance, he came home a little earlier than usual and instead of heading straight for his apartment, walked to where Harry and Sabrina were sitting and painting. He had more artists' equipment, including an easel, which he set awkwardly in front of Harry before making to walk away again.

"Jah, it's nothing, don't make a big deal of it," he said brushing away Harry's effusive thanks.

"No, son, it is a big deal, thank you," said Harry, unable to hide his delight. "Sabrina and I have been balancing the sketch book against trees, on tables with books shoved behind it, on just about anything we can find. Now, with an easel, we can do so much more."

"Jah, whatever, as I tuned you, it's no biggie," and he turned to walk away. Then, almost on an impulse, he turned and walked back to them. "Maybe now you'll do some painting of your own. From what I remember, yous a pretty lekker artist." Without waiting for Harry to reply, he turned on his heel and walked briskly away.

Harry watched the retreating figure of his son, his face perplexed.

"That uncle of yours, Sabrina, he's a funny one, isn't he? Don't know if I'll ever figure him out." He smiled and shook his head from side-to-side before setting the sketch pad onto the easel and pushing Sabrina's wheelchair up to it. "This, my girl, is an easel, and now we're really going to have fun!" Sabrina gurgled happily.

"So are we ever going to talk about what happened with Natalie?" asked Harry, gathering the courage to broach the subject. He'd cooked dinner, a simple spaghetti bolognaise, one of two dishes, along with macaroni and cheese, that he could competently make on his own, and when Calvin made to dish up and leave, he urged him to stay and eat with them.

"What's there to fuckin' talk about?" said Calvin, throwing down his fork and looking at his father.

"There's no need to swear, son."

"There's every fuckin' reason to swear when you keep getting in my face!"

"We're concerned about you, can't you see that?"

"Concerned 'bout me? What the hell for? I'm doin' just lekker. If anything, I dodged a bullet. You should be celebrating with me." And he picked up his fork to carry on eating.

"Bullshit!" said Talia, looking at him through narrowed eyes.

"Talia," said Harry, gently resting a hand on her arm.

"I call bullshit!" Talia repeated.

"Talia, you scheme you know so fuckin' much, why don't you get your own shit together before poking your fuckin' nose in my business! I don't need this shit." And Calvin pushed back his chair and made to pick up his plate and leave.

"Calvin, please!" Harry's voice was firm. "Just sit down. We won't talk about it if that's what you want, but you can't just keep shutting us down every time we try to talk to you. We're a family, maybe a little broken, as you've said so yourself, but a family all the same. What Talia and I are trying to say is that we care about you and are here for you."

Calvin sighed, slammed his plate noisily onto the table and sat down again.

"Jah, well that's all you had to tune me in the first place." And he put his head down and carried on eating in silence.

CHAPTER TWENTY-SIX

Cape Town 1930

WHEN KHALED DIED, there was much talk among the family about what would become of Sharifa. The male relatives thought it would be best if the house was sold and she moved in with one of the older aunts and uncles. But Sharifa was adamant. She would stay in her own home.

Auntie Yasmin and Uncle Sameer spoke in her defence; they lived next door, they reasoned, and would be right there if she needed any help. Auntie Bibi hmphed her disapproval. A woman living alone. It wasn't right, she'd muttered. But Auntie Yasmin could be persuasive when she wanted to be, and it was clear from Sharifa's determined jaw that she wasn't going anywhere.

So it was decided that Sharifa would stay, and Uncle Sameer would be her guardian. Though even as Uncle Majid, the eldest of the uncles, pronounced it, Yasmin and Sharifa exchanged a look and the twinkle in their eyes was not lost on Uncle Sameer. He smiled good naturedly, knowing full well who would be in charge.

Sharifa was so happy in her new arrangement that she would sometimes feel guilty. To come and go when she wanted, to not be anxious and fearful that she would do the wrong thing, say the wrong thing or, Allah forbid, have the dinner on the table five minutes late!

She ate porridge for dinner on some nights and if she wanted to get up in the middle of the night and read, which she was starting to do more and more, she could do so. And she didn't have to wander through to the cold, fireless kitchen, she could turn on a paraffin lamp and read right there in bed.

She had been a part of the Moslem Women's Society since she fell pregnant with Ali and, with Auntie Yasmin's help and support, was trying to encourage literacy classes among the women in the community. She'd helped persuade a young school teacher to come to the society hall once a week and teach basic reading and writing and attendance was encouraging – and growing all the time.

The only challenge was the expense of maintaining her home.

She talked it over one evening with Auntie Yasmin as they stood side-by-side in the kitchen chopping vegetables for the soup kitchen the next day. There was a young woman who came to the soup kitchen on Fridays, Auntie Yasmin said. Exceptionally tall, with flawless skin and eyes the colour of honey. Sharifa had noticed her, always sitting alone, and although she'd wanted to talk to her, there had never been the right opportunity. She'd been asking a lot of questions about the literacy classes, said Auntie Yasmin. And then her voice fell. She had left the home she and her husband shared with her in-laws, but her own family had refused to take her in, saying it was shameful and she should return. Her place was with her husband now.

"Everyone could see the bruises," Auntie Yasmin closed her eyes and took a deep breath. She opened them again. "I had asked the cobbler's wife to help find her a job, and she starts on Monday. Once she has a little money, I'm sure she will be happy to contribute to expenses."

"Isn't she the one they say is possessed by a jinn?" asked Uncle Sameer, looking up over his glasses from his newspaper. "The men at Mosque say she casts spells, love potions, that sort of thing."

"Huh! They would say that!" snorted Auntie Yasmin, throwing the chopping knife she was using down on the table and turning to him with her hands on her hips. "She's beautiful, and they're going to want an excuse when their wives see their eyes wandering! Spells! I've never heard such nonsense. That's the problem with you men," and she took up the knife again to point it at him, "a woman is brave enough to speak out and do something when she's being beaten black and blue by her husband, and suddenly she's possessed!"

"I didn't say anything!" Uncle Sameer raised one palm, his newspaper crumpling. "I'm merely telling you what the others say."

"Well, you can tell 'the others' that if they keep their eyes and their minds on Allah when they're at the Mosque, they should be immune to her 'spell'!"

And Sharifa chuckled.

When the young woman came to the soup kitchen the following week, Auntie Yasmin introduced her to Sharifa. She couldn't have been more than 18, but she held herself in such a way that she looked much older. Sharifa could only imagine she had seen much more than anyone her age should see.

"Sharifa, this is Marriyam, Marriyam, this is my daughter, Sharifa," and Sharifa looked at her Aunt and smiled.

"Hello, Marriyam, I believe you're working at the cobbler's, how is that going?" asked Sharifa.

"It's going well, thank you, Auntie, I am happy for the work and I'm learning a lot." She held out her delicate palms, red and calloused, for them to see. "My hands don't always thank me for it, though," and she smiled.

"I'm sure it will get easier," said Sharifa.

"It will," said Marriyam with a quick, firm nod of her head.

"I heard you may be looking for a place to stay."

"I need that more than anything," said Marriyam, and her eyes darkened as she said it.

"Where are you living now?"

"People in the community take me in, one or two nights at a time. But no one wants to be lumbered with the responsibility – or the shame – for too long. I spent one night on the docks, I've never been more frightened in my life and couldn't wait for day light to come."

Sharifa put out a hand and stroked the young woman's arm.

"Do you have any belongings?"

"I have a bag containing a few clothes, my Koran, and," she hesitated, "I have my crystals."

"Your crystals?" Sharifa's brow furrowed.

"My grandmother was a traveller, and she left me her collection of crystals when she died. They guide me and protect me and are my link to my grandmother whom I loved more than anyone in the world." Suddenly she sounded every bit a very young woman, longing for the security and the comfort of home. "Perhaps you've heard the way people talk about me? That I am a witch, or possessed by a jinn?"

Sharifa mumbled a protest but Marriyam continued. "Crystals aren't witchery, they aren't spells. They're our connection to the Earth and the sky. My Koran and my crystals are my most valued possessions, they are the two parts of me that make me whole, and nothing will persuade me to part with either of them."

Sharifa admired her conviction and nodded. "I have no problem with that, I know there are many things we do not understand in this world, Allah's abiding grace, even in the face of our worst sins, is certainly one of them." And she smiled sadly. "You need a place to stay, and I need help to keep living in my home, so I'd like to offer you a room in my house, if you would accept?"

Marriyam put her hands to her face and when she removed them, her eyes were filled with tears. "Thank you," she said in a quiet voice. "I don't know how to thank you."

"There's no need to thank me, my child. We are all Allah's children and we must help each other where we can. For as long as you live with me I promise to provide you a safe and secure roof over your head and a bed to sleep on. In return I will ask for a modest monthly rent, we can discuss how much you can afford on your pay, and help with the daily cooking and the other household chores. I would ask that you respect me by not bringing strangers into my house without my permission, and I do not want the world to know my business, so I would urge you to keep my home and what goes on in it private."

"Auntie, there's no danger of me talking out of turn to anyone, no one talks to me anyway," the young woman said sadly, and Sharifa smiled.

"Me neither, my dear child."

Marriyam had not exaggerated. She had one small bag which contained all her belongings, and the first thing Sharifa did was go through all her own clothing to pull out sets of shalwar kameez and nightgowns for her.

"I hope you don't take offence, but I have more than I need and would like you to have these," she said handing the pile of clothing to Marriyam. "They'll probably all be too short for you, but they're a start."

She would have the boys' room, and Sharifa's heart was happy to think of the room her beloved sons once slept in being occupied again. She stood at the door of the room that first day, watching Marriyam unpack her meagre belongings and set her Koran on the small table by the bed, and she felt her heart flip flopping – sorrow for the pain the young woman, and indeed all of them, had born, happiness that she'd help her find home.

CHAPTER TWENTY-SEVEN

Sharifa 1954

IF YOU SIT long enough with your sadness, my dear Rudo, you learn to make a companion of it. You find ways for it to fill the hollows, to seep into the empty spaces. Before long you feel whole again, complete. But filled with sorrow. That is where I was, dear Rudo, when I realised I had lost everyone I loved. That was when Marriyam came into my life.

Marriyam was a warrior. While I'd taken my sorrow and given it a warm, cosy place to live, Marriyam had beaten hers into arrows which she kept in a sheath across her chest to fight off enemies. But she never let the sorrow harden her. There was still so much love and hope in that young woman, who had every right to have given up on both. Which is why I think she had such an effect…on me, as well as the other young women who came to the Mosque.

We started the classes very slowly at first, pretending they were Koran lessons rather than English lessons. We would help the young teacher who was taking the classes by looking through books for hours on end in the library, trying to find material. At first no one came, and those who did, did it without the knowledge of their families. They were nervous, but they still came.

I remembered Father Patrick asking that very first day in class, "Why have you come here?" And I wanted to ask them too. I think most had not thought it through; they wanted something better, for themselves and for their families, but they may not have been able to put it into words.

Maybe they were scared to admit they wanted more, because what more should a good Moslem woman want but to be a good wife and mother and housekeeper, and carry the tenets of Islam with her in her heart and in her actions?

When, I wondered, did those things become so disjointed. When did it become so that you either had to be a good Moslem wife, or a woman of knowledge and respect? I sifted through the Koran, day in and day out, and could find nothing but praise for women, nothing but respect. My Uncle Ibrahim had confirmed this. So where did the women's fear of becoming more come from, I would ask myself. And I realised they came from within. Whereas my sorrow was putty to fill in the spaces, and Marriyam's was an arrow to fight off adversity, others had let theirs settle into doubt. Sadness and disappointment had made them feel small.

What we saw happen in class was so much more than learning how to read and write. We saw the women grow. And once again I'm reminded of my Auntie Anisa's words: what could be more threatening to a man fighting his own smallness than a woman growing before his very eyes? A small man is an angry man, her words come back to me all the time.

Our classes grew so big we had to start turning people away, and that was when some of the women joined the classes at the church. They spoke of an elderly priest named Father Patrick, and his assistant, a kind man with sandy coloured hair streaked with grey and startling green eyes.

CHAPTER TWENTY-EIGHT

Cape Town 1930

"AUNTIE, I'VE HEARD you pacing in the night, are you having trouble sleeping?" asked Marriyam after they'd done their dawn prayers together and begun to prepare tea and breakfast.

"I've never been a great sleeper, dear child, I hope I don't keep you awake with my activity?"

"No, no, nothing like that. But I'd like to give you a crystal to help you sleep, if you would accept it?"

"A crystal? I'd never thought about it before. What kind of crystal and what must I do?"

"Don't worry, nothing funny, you just put it under your pillow when you sleep. It will help relax you, take away your anxiety and help you sleep. Wait here."

Marriyam hurried to her room and came back with a dark, wooden box. She placed it on the kitchen table and even on this gloomy wintery morning, Sharifa saw the box dance with light and colour as Marriyam lifted the lid.

Fascinated, Sharifa came and sat opposite her as she carefully took out a small stone, bright white and iridescent. As she held it in her hand it seemed to take on the qualities of water, the light shifting inside it like the surface of the sea.

"This is moonstone. As the name suggests, it is connected to the night and brings tranquillity. It will take away your anxiety and help you sleep."

"It's beautiful," said Sharifa.

"Here, you can hold it." Marriyam passed it to Sharifa and she held it up in the palm of her hand and looked closely at it.

"It looks like the moon," said Sharifa. "It is well named."

Sharifa took it to her room and placed it under her pillow that night. The effect wasn't immediate, but over days and weeks she felt her mind settle more easily when she crawled into bed each night, and soon found herself sleeping longer and more comfortably.

It became the two women's evening ritual after dinner, sitting together at the kitchen table, the wood fire lit and water boiling for their tea, and examining the crystals.

Sharifa was amazed how much Marriyam knew about stones, and her incredible natural gift for healing.

"These tiny stones hold all the world's power of healing inside them," Marriyam would whisper reverently, picking up an amethyst and rolling it in her palm. "They connect with our energy channels, taking away the negative and allowing the positive energy to flow into our body. So small, but filled with vibrations which we feel deep inside us, without even realising."

"And this one?" Sharifa asked, delicately picking up a smooth, amber coloured one, scored through with darker rings.

"That's tiger eye, for harmony." And Marriyam covered

the stone in Sharifa's palm with her own and looked at the older woman with a smile, deep set with emotion.

Afterwards, Sharifa always regretted not urging Marri-yam to carry the black obsidian for protection.

CHAPTER TWENTY-NINE

2015

"SO IT'S THE Valentine's Day dance at the Club on Saturday, what do you say?"

Harry, Clayton and Sabrina were in their usual spot on the veranda and Harry was helping Sabrina drink water from a sippy cup. The air was hot and thick, building up to rain, and Harry knew that even though she resisted him, he had to make her drink.

"What do I say about what?" said Harry, looking up at his friend from under furrowed brows.

"What do you say we go together?"

"As Valentines? Clayton, you know I love you, but I'm not going to the dance as your date! Besides, what would Ruby say?" And they both chuckled.

"Ah, Harry, my old friend, you know everyone goes to the dance, those who have dates and those who are looking for dates!" And he winked.

"Are you starting this nonsense again?" Harry closed his eyes and shook his head.

"What nonsense?" asked Clayton, raising his palms on either side of him in mock defence.

"Honestly, Clayton, when will you get this into your thick skull? I am not dating – not now, not ever!"

"So how do I look?" Harry was fiddling with his bow tie, holding on to either side of it and wiggling it up and down.

Talia put her finger and her thumb to her mouth and let out a long whistle.

"Well look at you! Don't you look handsome!" She was beaming.

"Do you really think so?" Harry was running his hands over his head, trying to get his hair to lie down over the bald patch.

"Yes, I really think so."

"That damn Clayton, getting it into his head that I need to get out, go dancing! I really don't know how I let him trick me into doing this!"

"He's right, Dad, you do need to get out more, you spend all day, all night, cooped up in this house, looking after Sabrina. It's about time you went out and had some fun."

"I'm quite happy here at home, with Sabrina. I get to do with her all I missed out on doing with you and Clayton and Bernice when you needed me." And he looked down at the ground. They were both silent. Then he lifted his eyes and saw the emotion reflected in hers.

"We've never spoken about it, Sabrina, and so I've never had the chance to say I'm sorry for how I let you down." She stopped him with a raised hand and a little shake of her head.

"You don't need to do this, Dad."

"Yes, I do. I want to tell you how much I love you and how much I regret I wasn't there for you."

"You're here for us, and for Sabrina, now, and that's what matters. The rest is in the past, and better left alone."

Harry walked over to her, put his arms around her and held her tight.

Then he drew in his breath and pulled away. "I'm too old to be gadding about."

"What gadding about?" Talia swallowed her emotion and smiled at him. "This is the Club Valentine Dance, everyone and their mother will be there – literally. It's not the Ritz Hotel!"

"You should be the one going out, not me."

"I don't have the energy to get dressed up and go to no dance, Dad. I really have no interest in it, not at this stage in my life anyway. I'm too tired. You go and enjoy yourself and Sabrina and I will watch Dirty Dancing for the 100th time. You know it's our favourite!" She took a step forward and kissed him on the cheek. Her voice was steady and serious. "You look great, go out and live for the present for a change, instead of mourning about the past."

She let go of him and walked towards the lounge to sit with Sabrina and as he turned to leave he said, quietly under his breath so she didn't hear him, "The past, my love, never really leaves us – and that's the blessing and the curse."

"This was a mistake," said Harry as they pulled into the dark parking lot of the Club. Clayton turned off the engine and they could feel the bass thumping through the car seats.

"Maybe you should take me home."

"What?" Clayton swivelled around in his seat to look at his friend. "We did not get all dapper and dressed up to go home and watch the box! Besides, look how excited your sister is!"

Ruby had already stepped out of the car and Harry looked over at her, squeezed into a too-tight red velour dress, her hair done up that afternoon by Stella Rodriguez who did the hair for all the ladies on the block for the Valentine's dance. Her eyes were shining behind her glasses.

Harry let out a sigh. "OK."

Clayton hit the steering wheel with the heel of his hand and smiled. "Then what are we waiting for?" He opened his door, stepped out and swung it shut, then came around to Harry's side of the car and with Ruby on his arm, they walked together across the dark car park towards the crowded steps.

"I don't have a good feeling about this," said Harry.

A slight boy with peroxide streaks through his dark hair, no more than 12 or 13, saw them coming and quickly stamped out his cigarette before shouting to the others and shoving them out the way, "Oeuns! Move out the way! Make room for the balis!" He turned to them. "Howzit Uncles, howzit Auntie."

"Melvyn," said Clayton, pausing on the steps and cocking his head to one side. "Does your grandmother know you're out?"

"Yes, Uncle, I tuned – I told – her."

"And how about your smoking? Does she know about that?"

An equally slight boy next to Melvyn started to laugh

behind his hand.

"Not a sound from you, Ivon Greenland!" Clayton turned on the offender. "I could smell the cigarette smoke on you all the way from the car!"

"Sorry, Uncle." They both hung their heads.

"Don't say sorry to me! Say sorry to your grandmother! That fine woman works day and night to put food on the table and send you to school, and this is how you thank her?"

"No, Uncle," they said in unison, shaking their heads.

"This is how it starts! Today you're sneaking cigarettes, tomorrow you're doing drugs! Is that how you want to live your lives?"

"No, Uncle." They were looking down at their untied trainers.

"Well, then, stop loitering with these delinquents," and Clayton swept his hand across the crowd of older boys and girls occupying the steps, "and go inside! Or I will tell your grandmother! Is that what you want?"

"No, Uncle!" They looked up at him, their eyes wide.

"Then go in!" He gestured impatiently towards the door and they stumbled up the steps, jostling each other to get away first, and disappeared into the dark doorway of the hall.

Harry started to chuckle.

"Still bullying poor, innocent little children, I see. You should pick on someone your own size!"

Clayton looked around sternly then broke into a smile. "Bullying indeed! Can't have them getting up to the same nonsense we did when we were their age, can we, old friend?" He poked Harry in the ribs.

"They must have shat themselves when they saw you coming up the steps."

Clayton hmphed. "Did you see their jeans? I could see their whole underpants!"

"You sound a thousand years old right now!" Harry laughed. "This is why we should be at home with a blanket on our laps in front of the telly, and leave the partying to the lighties."

"Ha! What do the lighties know about partying? Nothing! We'll show them how to party! Now, you old codger, do you remember any of the old dance moves, or do I have to teach them to you all over again?"

"I'll leave the jiving to you, Clayton, as I always did. I had two left feet then and I have two left feet now."

"And yet, somehow, you still got all the women," said Clayton rolling his eyes.

"Don't start that nonsense again!" And they both started laughing.

Ruby had gone on ahead and they found her at a table with eight other women, all wearing similarly tight, bright dresses and chatting loudly to each other over the music. Earlier that day, as they'd all sat in Glynnis Green's lounge waiting for Stella to do their hair, Ruby had filled them in about Harry joining them at the dance, and they'd all been waiting eagerly to see him.

"That brother of yous was damn fine in his day, Rube," said Glynnis, her hand on her hip and waving one finger in the air. "I wouldn't mind a little bump and grind with him!" And she started moving her hips suggestively back and forth to raucous laughter from the others.

Harry was aware of the looks and whispers as they walked towards the table, but kept his gaze fixed on Clayton's back, never more grateful than now for his friend's confident swagger. He took Clayton's lead when he went around the table greeting each woman by name and tried to avoid their gaping stares.

They sat down next to each other at one end of the table, and Harry started to relax.

The old hall brought back a lifetime of memories, some good, some not so good, but all with a sense of familiarity Harry realised was missing from so many aspects of his life. He was pretty sure those were the same heart-shaped Styrofoam table decorations they'd hauled out every year for Valentine's Day all those decades ago, and these were sure as hell the same tables and chairs. He lifted the worn white table cloth and started looking behind the table leg closest to him to see if he could find where he and Clayton had carved their names with a pocket knife when they weren't much older than Melvyn and Ivon.

"Looking for our names?" Clayton shouted at him over the music. "Don't bother. I've checked every table in here! They either tossed it out or sanded it over. But we could always do some fresh ones!" He winked at Harry.

"And how will you lecture the poor youth of Somerset about morality when you're doing nonsense yourself?"

Clayton shoved his friend lightly on the arm and they laughed, just as the two friends would have laughed together all those years ago.

The hip hop track ended, and when the next number on the playlist was a waltz, Clayton couldn't sit still any longer.

"If you'll excuse me, ladies," he said, standing up and bowing slightly, "I'm going to take my lovely lady for a spin." He held out his hand and Ruby stood up and took it, giggling and blushing like a schoolgirl. Harry watched them walk away, arm in arm, and smiled. He saw Nani Sharifa's dimpled smile in his imagination, and he grew pensive.

He could still remember how it felt when his beloved Nani was so sick those last few months. To watch her not being able to get out of bed on her own, and not see her waiting for them in the garden after school. Despite the pain, she would always find the strength to smile at them. To hold out her arms and hug them tight. To tell them how much she loved them. On her good days, she would scoot over in her bed and pat the empty side and the children would jump on to it, careful to first take off their shoes or Gogo Rudo would shout.

"Would you like to look at the magic?" Nani would ask them. Her voice had turned gravelly, laboured like her breath.

"Yes, please, Nani!" they'd both cry out.

And she would slowly reach under her bed and pull out the box.

The last time they sat on her bed, Nani did an unexpected thing. She showed them each stone as she always did, and whispered what they represented, and then she set two in the palm of her hand, closed the box and put the rest away.

Her look was very serious, but still full of love.

She took the rose pink one, the one for love that always made Nani's eyes fill with shadows, and she handed it to Ruby.

"My darling Ruby, this one is for you. Find your love and hold on to it, no matter what." Her voice trembled slightly. She took a breath and carried on. "And this one, my darling Harry, this garnet is for you. This one is for blessings in your family, may you be blessed with children and with grandchildren who you will love and care for all the days of your life." Nani started coughing, the exertion had been too much, and Gogo Rudo had run in and chased the children off the bed and out the room.

They'd hovered at the door and seen Gogo Rudo holding Nani in her arms, gently rubbing her back until, slowly, the coughing subsided.

Ruby and Harry held the precious stones in their hands and lifted them up, marvelling how the light of the sun dipped and danced through them.

As much as he wanted his stone, something about it made Harry sad. Something told him that as long as Nani was alive, the stones belonged with her, in her box, only to be taken out to show them when they'd been very good. As young as he was, Harry felt both the burden and the sorrow of the stone in his hand, and knew at that moment that giving them the stones was Nani's way of saying goodbye.

"Hello, Uncle." Harry turned with a start and it took a moment for him to register that the young woman standing beside him was Natalie. "Sorry if I startled you."

He stood up. "Natalie, my dear, no not at all! I was miles away, just an old man dreaming of the past! I'm so happy to see you! How are you? And how is Tamara? We so enjoyed having her that evening…" his voice trailed off as they both remembered how the evening had ended.

"She's fine, exhaustingly full of life as always," said Natalie with a smile. "She started Grade One, so it's been a big adjustment for all of us."

"Wonderful news, just wonderful. I wish her all the best."

There was an awkward silence and then Harry heard Natalie take a deep breath and ask in what she hoped was as casual a manner as possible, belied by the sudden shrillness in her voice, "So how's everyone at the house?"

"Oh, everyone is just fine. And so is Calvin," he smiled.

"I'm that transparent, aren't I?" And she gave a sad smile.

He sat down and patted the chair next to him.

"Calvin is Calvin, pig-headed and unreasonable as always – but then you'd know that, wouldn't you, girl?"

"I don't understand him, I thought we were getting on really well, really getting somewhere – and then, just like that," and she snapped her fingers, "he gets a worm in his head and we're over."

Harry sighed. "Natalie, my girl, has Calvin told you much about himself, about our lives?"

"No, Uncle, not a lot; besides the odd comment here and there when he lets his guard down – or when he's had too much to drink. But people talk. You know what the community's like, people love to talk. So I've pieced a lot of it together."

"Imagine Calvin, not much older than your Tamara is now, witnessing something so horrific that he stopped speaking for over a year. Over a year! Did you know that?" Harry looked at her and she shook her head. "And then seeing his family ripped apart, and me, to all intents and purposes in the eyes of a child, abandoning him." Harry brought his right hand up and started rubbing his eyes hard, as if to erase the image.

"Uncle, I'm so sorry, I didn't mean to upset you." Natalie placed her hand on his arm and he stopped rubbing his eyes and looked at her.

"There's no need to apologise my girl, it's I who should apologise, for all the heartache I caused to the people I loved the most. What I'm trying to tell you, Natalie, is that Calvin is deeply wounded by his past, and I don't know if he will ever heal. He's over 40, and no one can really help him but himself – and I'm not sure if he wants to.

"But this is no talk for a beautiful night like tonight! It's the Valentine's Day dance, you should be enjoying yourself! Who did you come with, girl?"

"A bunch of my girlfriends who were tired of seeing me mope around looking miserable and persuaded me to come out – but I'm not sure I want to be here."

"Well, that makes two of us!" laughed Harry. "I'm here with my sister and brother-in-law. Clayton's my oldest friend and he more or less dragged me here kicking and screaming! Ah, speak of the devil and he's sure to appear," Harry smiled and pointed to Clayton and Ruby coming off the dance floor hand-in-hand and walking towards them.

"Just as it's always been, you old dog, I leave you alone for five minutes and you're surrounded by beautiful women," Clayton put out his hand to Natalie and she took it. "Clayton Bent, my dear," he said with a little bow, "The best dancer in Somerset, but then Harry has probably already told you that."

"No, Clayton, it may surprise you to know we had better things to talk about than you," smiled Harry. "This is Natalie Ismail."

"I can't imagine what – ah, Natalie, Calvin's friend, it's a pleasure to meet you. And this is Ruby, my dear wife," he stepped back and made way for Ruby to come forward.

"Hellos," said Ruby squinting up at Natalie. "My hearing's shot, what's your name?" Natalie leaned in close and said her name again. "Who's your father, girl?"

"Anthony Ismail," Natalie replied.

"What was that?"

"Anthony Ismail!" Natalie shouted into her ear.

"Oh, Ismail, the Somerset Ismails?"

"Yes, that's right," nodded Natalie.

"Nice to meet you, girl."

"Well, I guess I'd better go and join my friends, they'll be wondering where I got to. I'm happy to have seen you, Uncle," she said, looking intently at Harry, "and thank you for the talk. Nice to have met you both." She gave a little wave to Clayton and Ruby and turned and walked away.

"Pretty girl, that," said Clayton.

"Bright as a button, too," said Harry. "I reckon she's exactly what Calvin needs in his life; pity he's letting her slip through his fingers."

"Calvin's here," Clayton came back to the table to report to Harry. He'd been walking to the bar to look for drinks when he'd seen Calvin standing against a wall with a woman. He had one arm wrapped around her waist and was holding a bottle by the neck with the other.

He'd raised the bottle in greeting when he'd spotted Clayton and called out good naturedly to him.

"Hey, Uncle Clay! Having a lekker jol?"

Clayton walked over. "Yes, Calvin, having a great time. I'm here with Harry."

"You're here with my o'man? Sweet!" He slurred.

"Are you going to come over and say hi to your Dad and Aunt Ruby?"

"Hey, Uncle Clay, I'd like to, but as you can check, I have my hands full," and he jerked his chin in the direction of the woman and smiled his lop-sided smile. The woman, who Clayton didn't recognise, looked over her shoulder, as if noticing the older man standing there for the first time.

"OK, Calvin, you take care of yourself," and he patted him lightly on his upper arm before walking away.

"What's he up to?" asked Harry.

"The usual, I'm afraid."

Harry sighed.

"Now, now, old friend, he's a grown man and there's nothing you can do. And maybe that's the hardest part of all."

The commotion started just as Harry had turned to Clayton to tell him he was ready to leave. It hadn't been a bad evening, but he was tired and the noise and the smoke was beginning to give him a headache.

Clayton and Ruby had spent most of the evening on the dancefloor and were both tired too. They were getting ready to say their goodbyes when they heard the raised voices, followed by a crash of furniture. Everyone stopped dancing and a crowd started forming at the back of the hall.

"A fight. Typical to mess up a nice evening like this," said Clayton with a shake of his head. "Let's get out of here." He took Ruby's arm and with Harry in tow started to lead the way out of the hall.

As they passed a group near the door, Harry thought he heard Calvin's name and stopped walking.

"Clay, I think it's Calvin." Harry grabbed Clayton's arm to stop him.

"What?" he turned to his friend.

"I think Calvin's part of the commotion."

Clayton sighed. "OK, you wait here with Rube, I'll go and check it out."

But Harry couldn't stand back, not knowing, and found Ruby a chair near the door and started walking towards the scene of the fight.

"Excuse me, excuse me," he gently pushed past people to get to the front, and when he finally did, there was Calvin tussling with another man. They were surrounded by a ring of spectators, egging them on, and Harry could see, even from a distance, that Calvin's eyes were glazed, blind with alcoholic strength and rage.

That was when he saw Natalie, standing a little to the side, her face in her hands, surrounded by a group of friends.

"Natalie, Natalie, what's going on, what are they fighting about?" he yelled over the noise.

"Oh Uncle!" Natalie started to cry when she saw him. "I was dancing with Dexter, an old friend from high school, when suddenly Calvin came out of nowhere and started yelling at him and throwing punches. I tried to stop him, but Dexter was in a fighting mood and the two of them just started beating up on each other. I don't know what to do!"

"There's nothing you can do, my girl, just wait here."

Harry was feeling unsteady on his feet and wished he'd brought his walking stick, but he had to get to Calvin, had to stop him before something terrible happened. Nani's words came back to him and if he wasn't so anxious, he may have smiled – the blessing of family.

He skirted around the crowd and drew closer to the pair, calling out to Calvin and trying to catch his eye. At that moment Calvin lunged at his opponent and, using the force of his body, threw him across the floor. Dexter stumbled and fell and Calvin was on top of him, hitting him repeatedly in the face.

"Calvin, stop! Please stop!" Harry pleaded.

Clayton saw him and started heading in his direction calling frantically out to him.

"Harry, get away from there! Leave them alone, you'll get hurt!"

As he said it, the two men were on their feet again and circling each other. Harry had taken another step towards Calvin, arms out and entreating him to stop, but neither of the men were paying any attention. Calvin shoved Dexter hard in the chest and, as he stumbled backwards and to the ground, he took Harry down with him.

By this stage the DJ had stopped the music and the whole room heard the thud as Harry fell.

Calvin was staring incredulously at his father lying on the ground, too stunned to move as the crowd pushed forward and past him to get to Harry's side.

Clayton shoved past him, throwing him an angry look, and ran to his friend.

"Harry, Harry, are you OK? Speak to me, my old friend!"

"I'm OK, I'm OK," he was trying to sit up but people were urging him to lie still till they could assess his injuries. "I'm OK but I think I've hurt my leg."

Clayton could see that his friend was in pain.

"Just lie still, Harry, wait for the paramedics, we'll soon have you right as rain," said Clayton in his cheeriest tone.

The police arrived before the paramedics, and Harry, lying on the floor with Ruby clucking concernedly on one side and Clayton trying to placate the situation on the other, looked over at Calvin. He was standing completely limp, putting up no fight as the six policemen summoned from the local station swarmed around him, grabbing his wrists to snap rusty handcuffs around them, all yelling at him at once and shoving him towards the door. Moments before he was pushed out of sight, swallowed up by the thickening crowd, Calvin looked back and the two men's eyes met.

CHAPTER THIRTY

Sharifa 1932

MY DARLING ALI, Marriyam is becoming like a daughter to me, the daughter I never had, and how I wish she could have met my boys. She is a version of myself I wish I'd known, had it not been dead 30 years. She is fearless and sure of her place in the world. She is resolute in her faith and the powers of Allah, but also aware of the power and strength within her, deeply grounded and earthly. We spend every morning and evening together, praying and talking and learning about crystals. She helps at the Mosque on her days off work and attends the English classes when she can, and I see her talking to the other young women and instilling in them the same sense of self-worth that seems to come so naturally to her. I can not understand how she can be so brave, so confident, so optimistic after all she has seen and experienced in her young life. But it gives me strength, my dear son – and hope. I wish for her what I wish for you and Mohammed too: a life full of love, guided by faith and fulfilled by family. I wish her and you immense happiness, you deserve nothing less.

Marriyam would leave for work just before sunrise each morning, and, if the cobbler had been busy, only get home long after dark. The two women would pray together each morning before Marriyam ate a quick breakfast and headed out, and Sharifa would spend the rest of the morning quietly sorting the laundry before leaving for the soup kitchen to help with lunch.

One morning, about two months after Marriyam moved in, Sharifa was in the courtyard, bent over the tub and scrubbing linen, when she heard a knock at the door.

She stood up stiffly and dusted off her knees, then covered her head with a scarf and went to open the door.

Two heavy-set, elderly women in full hijab stood in the doorway.

"As Salaam Alaikum." Sharifa nodded slightly.

"Wa Alaikum Salaam," said the taller of the two. "I am Mrs. Ayoob, the senior, and this is Mrs. Ayoob junior."

Sharifa smiled at the introduction.

"And how may I help you?"

"May we come in?" said Mrs. Ayoob senior.

"Yes, of course." Sharifa opened the door wider and indicated the way to the small living room to the right of the house.

"Shukraan." They walked past her and sat side-by-side on the two-seater sofa. Sharifa pulled a wooden chair with a tall back through from the kitchen and sat in front of them.

"We are Marriyam's aunties," said Mrs. Ayoob.

"Her aunties?"

"Well, her husband's aunties, so her aunties by marriage," added the younger Ayoob sister, her hands folded in her lap, dusty, slippered feet crossed at the ankles and dangling just above the floor.

"I see." Sharifa was starting to feel uneasy.

"We have been sent by Marriyam's mother-in-law, at the request of her son, Nabil, to discuss with you, as a fellow Moslem woman, how together we can find a solution to the disgrace Marriyam has brought upon our family." The older Mrs. Ayoob had taken up the conversation again and her sister shook her head and muttered under her breath as she spoke.

"Disgrace?" asked Sharifa, her brows furrowed.

"You should see her mother-in-law, Wallah! A broken woman!" And she hit her forehead with the heel of her hand. "She can't bear to be seen in public, for shame. She won't even go to Masjid!" Now her sister was vehemently shaking her head and mumbling loudly.

"I'm not sure I understand…"

"The whole community is talking about her, how her daughter-in-law is possessed by a jinn, Hafizna Allah!" And her sister cupped her cheeks with her hands and shook her head from side-to-side. "The whole community says the family is cursed and she must return in order to set things right again."

Satisfied that they'd said all that was necessary, the two sisters sat back, hands folded in their laps.

Sharifa paused, and shook her head slowly as if trying to understand. "Forgive me if I'm speaking out of turn, but Marriyam left because she was being beaten by her husband." She spoke slowly but pointedly. "She left for her own protection."

"Wallah!" cried the older sister again. "How can you say such a thing? Her place is with her husband. He is her protector. How can she hope for protection out on the streets?"

"She is not out on the streets, she is living here, with me, in my house." Sharifa again spoke slowly, trying her best to control her emotions.

The younger sister creased her eyes into what she hoped would be a smile. "With all due respect, two single women living alone is not proper. It is haraam."

"It is haraam to beat one's wife." And now there was no disguising her anger. "Or perhaps we should consult an Imam on that. My uncle is an Imam and would be happy to discuss this with us. Would you like us to go to him together now?" She stood up.

The two women hmphed in unison and the older Ayoob looked at her sister.

"Sister, I think we were mistaken, we will not find any help here and we should leave." She put her hands on either side of her and rocked back and forth till she shuffled to the edge of the sofa and pushed herself upright. Her sister followed suit with equal gracelessness. They both paused a moment to catch their breath.

"We have to say we are disappointed," said the senior Mrs. Ayoob, clasping her chubby hands over her belly. "We thought we could appeal to your sense of decency, as a fellow Moslem woman. But perhaps we should not be surprised. After all, a woman who puts notions into other women's heads about reading and writing and other ways of taking them away from their rightful place in the home is not a woman who we could count on for help. We see we will have to approach matters a different way." She paused pointedly before continuing. "Marriyam will return to her married home, of that you can be certain."

They headed for the door and Sharifa watched them leave, too filled with anger and shock to move. But as she gathered her thoughts and finally managed to control her breathing, the gravity of their thinly veiled threat began to sink in and through the anger and shock was the much more powerful emotion of fear.

"The Koran clearly states that the relationship between a husband and wife must be based on tranquillity, unconditional love, tenderness, protection, encouragement, peace, kindness, comfort, justice and mercy," said Uncle Ibrahim, his hands busy with his prayer beads as he spoke.

"There is no ambiguity, the prophet himself says of a husband towards his wife: Give her food when you take food, clothe her when you clothe yourself, do not revile her, and do not beat her."

"And what of women learning to read and write, Uncle?"

"Once again, the Koran speaks about women having an equal right to acquire knowledge or be educated in order to assume the status of righteous people endowed with the knowledge and understanding that leads to the obedience of Allah in all aspects of life – spiritual and physical."

"Then why do so many people object when a woman refuses to be treated as lesser?" asked Sharifa.

"Because they are afraid. And if only they would trust in Allah and follow his directives, they would see there is no need to be."

Uncle Ibrahim was her father's oldest brother and an Imam, and Sharifa remembered being afraid of him as a child, with his thick, black beard and booming big voice. The years had softened his voice and his beard, turned white with age, and Sharifa had decided to seek his advice. The visit by Marriyam's aunties had shaken her, but she was still hesitant to act on it until, two days later, an incident took place at the Mosque that deeply troubled her.

Someone had broken into the room they used for their classes and stolen all their books and papers. Had they been stolen to help someone less fortunate to read and write, Sharifa wouldn't have minded. But the next day they found a pile of burnt papers, still smouldering, at the back by the boundary wall. And sifting through them were traces of one of their books on phonics.

CHAPTER THIRTY-ONE

2015

"NO, I'M NOT going to press charges, how ridiculous! He's my son and, besides, he didn't mean to hurt me." Harry was lying in traction on the narrow hospital bed with Clayton on one side and Talia on the other.

"This is what you do, you excuse him! You're always finding excuses for him!" Talia's voice was shrill.

"I'm not excusing him, Talia, but I'm also not going to go to court and see my own son charged! Besides, I should imagine a weekend in our local jail has been punishment enough!"

"I love him, you know I do, Dad, and I'm so grateful for all he's done. Giving Sabrina and me a home, helping us bring you home, but he's out of control, he's a danger to himself and everyone around him. And you have to stop enabling him, through some misguided sense of guilt or responsibility!"

"Give him time, Talia, give him time. We all need time."

"How much time, though, Dad? How much time is enough?"

Clayton stepped forward and put his arm around her shoulders.

"There, there, my girl," he said in a soothing voice. "Your Dad is a tough old goat, a lot tougher than he looks right now," he jerked his finger at the patient and smiled. "He's going to be fine, the doctor says it's just a hairline fracture, and he knows the right thing to do. So does Calvin, he just needs to find his way."

The next day, released from jail with a fine, Calvin showered and shaved and went to visit his father.

Harry was sleeping when he arrived and Calvin pulled up a chair close to the bed and sat fiddling with his hands until his father stirred and slowly opened his eyes.

"Hello, son."

"Howzit." Calvin glanced at him, then looked down again. "How ya feeling?"

"Not too bad, all things considered. Doc says I can come home tomorrow."

"Lekker." Calvin was looking down at his hands, fingertips touching, straightening them then bending them to make a tent shape. "I fucked up. I didn't check you there. Soz, OK?"

"Frankly I'm surprised to see you here," said Harry. Calvin looked up sharply. "The old Calvin would have run away for a week, not been seen or heard from by anyone – and then done more stupid stuff." Harry smiled out of the corner of his mouth and anyone watching would have seen it reflected in his son.

"Jah, well, I scheme I may be out of stupid stuff."

"That's very possible," Harry nodded.

"I had a span to drink, and then I saw that asshole with

Natalie – I guess I lost my cool."

"What do you care, son? You dodged a bullet with her, you said so yourself. So let her go, let her be with whoever she wants to be with. You have no right to throw her away but still try to keep the key."

"Jah, jah, whatever."

"Don't whatever me. Sometimes we need to hear the truth – and the truth hurts."

"Jah, well I didn't jol here for a lecture," Calvin stood up, "I joled to check how you were, to tune you I'm sorry and to aks if you need anything."

Harry sighed. "No, son, I don't need anything, thank you."

"Cool, then I'm gonna cut. I'll jol with Uncle Clay tomorrow to pick you up and take you cabin."

"Thank you, son."

"Laters." And he walked out the door.

Harry hardly slept that night. The hard hospital bed and the constant noise in the corridors was part of it, but the other part was his mind, which wouldn't stop going round and round, every thought circling him back to that day – and the look on Calvin's face after the gun was fired. And he realised with a start that while the rest of his son may have grown up, become a man – whatever that really meant – those were still the eyes of a very frightened little boy.

"You were damn lucky," said the doctor, his back to them, examining the x-ray on the viewing box. "I'm not even sure how you managed it, but there's hardly any damage at all –

even the hairline fracture seems to have fused."

"He's a tough old dog, what I've been telling everyone," said Clayton, slapping his knees and laughing.

"Takes one to know one," smiled Harry.

"Thank you, doctor, so I'm fine, I'm good to go?"

"Yes, perfectly fine. I'd recommend you're careful not to strain the leg too much or overdo it, at least for a couple of weeks. But, otherwise, carry on as normal."

"What a relief. Thank you, doctor."

Clayton retrieved Harry's walking stick from the floor and handed it to him, and the two men left the surgery and walked out into the hall. They were standing and waiting for the elevator when Harry saw Natalie. She was coming out of the diagnostic centre on the wing opposite to the doctor's surgery and walking towards them.

She noticed them standing there and hesitated, then carried on walking.

As she drew nearer Harry saw that her eyes were red and swollen.

"Natalie, my dear, how good to see you," said Harry.

"Oh, hello Uncle Harry, Uncle Clayton," she was smiling a little too brightly. "What are you doing here?"

"Oh, just getting the diagnosis on my old leg," Harry lifted it slightly off the ground."

"And?"

"The doctor's given me a clean bill of health, says I've healed completely!"

"He'll soon be back to running marathons," chuckled Clayton.

Natalie smiled. "That's wonderful news, I'm so happy to hear that."

"And you?" Harry asked cautiously. "All OK with you?"

"Yes, yes, all fine thanks…oh, please excuse me," she said, rummaging in her handbag, "I seem to have left my car keys behind, I'd better go get them – you go ahead, I'll catch the elevator on its way back up. Nice to have seen you both, please greet everyone for me." As she hurried off, Harry saw her car keys dangling off a clip attached to her handbag, but said nothing.

"What are you saying?" asked Talia.

"I'm not saying anything. I'm just telling you what I saw. She was coming out of the diagnostics centre and she looked like she'd been crying, that's all," said Harry.

He and Talia were sitting at the kitchen table having a cup of tea. Sabrina was in her wheelchair at Harry's side. Every now and then he would blow on the tea in her plastic sippy cup before putting it to her lips and tipping it. Sometimes a little of the sweet, milky tea would dribble down her chin and Harry would reach for a facecloth beside him and gently wipe it off.

"Look, it could have been anything, a urinary tract infection, for example," said Talia, waving a hand in the air.

"Why on earth a urinary tract infection?" asked Harry with a furrowed brow.

"I don't know! My point is, you can go to a diagnostic centre for any number of things – in fact, the list is endless."

"Yes," said Harry, tipping the last drops of tea into Sabrina's mouth, "it is."

"Clay, I'm conflicted." The pair were sitting on the veranda, watching the rain falling in sheets and all but obscuring the garden beyond, and Harry had to raise his voice to be heard over the drumming on the roof. "It's none of my business. Or is it?" He turned to his friend.

"You're right, it's none of your business," said Clayton.

"But?"

"No 'but', Harry. My advice is stay out of it."

"But what if she's pregnant, and what if it's Calvin's?"

"Which part of 'it's none of your business' don't you understand?" He looked straight at Harry. "You don't want to get yourself mixed up in this one. This one goes too deep. There could be a life involved."

"Which is exactly why I need to do something." Harry folded his arms across his chest.

"You really are a stubborn old goat, aren't you?" Clayton shook his head and smiled, then reached for his beer, threw back his head and took a long gulp.

Harry looked up at the massive steel and glass doors and hesitated. Family blessing. He saw Nani's dimpled smile again and took a deep breath before pulling the heavy front door open.

The silence of the reception area amplified the sound of his stick on the tiled floor and he regretted bringing it. He was beginning to regret all of it, but the receptionist had already spotted him and was intently watching him make his slow, steady progress across the entrance hall towards her desk.

He stepped up to the desk and she looked him up and down, and Harry was suddenly painfully aware of his clothes, which no amount of painstaking pressing could improve.

"Yes?" the woman looked at him over her turtle shell glasses.

"Good morning, I'm looking for Natalie Ismail."

"Do you have an appointment?"

"No, ma'am, I do not."

"And who should I say wishes to see her?"

"Mr. Rhoades. Mr. Harry Rhoades."

"Please could you take a seat and I'll speak to Ms. Ismail." She indicated an upright chair at the far end of the reception area and Harry nodded his head and walked away. He could hear her talking in hushed tones.

She put down the phone and waved her arm over her head at him. "Mr. Rhoades."

"Yes," Harry was already on his feet and walked as quickly as he could back to the reception desk.

"Ms. Ismail is out of the office. It would be best if you make an appointment next time."

Harry nodded, balancing both hands on the top of his walking stick and rocking back and forth on his heels. "Thank you, ma'am, for your kind assistance. I will do that." And he turned and walked slowly out the door, aware of every tap of his walking stick echoing in the silence, and back on to the noisy street.

Clayton was right, he thought to himself as he walked to the terminus to sit out the long wait for a minibus taxi that would take him home. It was none of his business.

Leila would always tell the children things had a way of working themselves out. We can worry and we can stress, she'd say, but there's only so much we can do. Wait, and it will be fine in the end. Maybe not the way you expected, but fine.

Harry used to wonder if his mother looked back on her life and thought it had all turned out fine, just as it should have, or if those were just words she used to make them feel better every time they were disappointed or sad that things hadn't worked out.

He imagined how lonely she must have been, never remarrying, devoting her whole life to making sure the children had everything they needed. He knew there were some very tough times and that there was some help from Uncle Mohammed, especially when school fees were due and his mother had no idea how she was going to raise them. But Uncle Mohammed wasn't the businessman Uncle Mustafa had been, and there wasn't a lot of spare cash available.

When Nani Sharifa came to live with them that summer, she brought a gold necklace given to her by her Auntie Yasmin at her Nikkah.

"It's not much, my sweet Leila, but I have nothing else to give, and I want you to have this, to do as you wish – to keep or to sell if you need the money."

Harry remembered Leila crying the day she sold it; it got them through another school term and that year they both had brand new school shoes for the first time. When Harry lost his pair two weeks into the term – left them at the side of the dam after they'd gone for an after-school dip – he didn't know how to tell his mother, and didn't cry when she gave him a hiding that evening. He deserved every smack, he told himself as he bit his lip to stop the tears. He had to go to school barefoot for a week, until Leila managed to buy a very worn second-hand pair from a neighbour.

Harry also remembered Leila's joy years later when she held Calvin in her arms for the first time. "He has your eyes – just like my dear father!" And even though Gwennie was quick to point out that she had green eyes on her side of the family too, Leila didn't let it dampen her excitement.

Gogo Rudo had died 10 years earlier, and Leila had thought about moving back to Salisbury, but when Harry announced that Gwennie was pregnant with their first child, she decided to stay.

"I want to be able to help look after my grandchildren, I want to see them grow up."

She finally moved off the plot, which, as the economic situation worsened and the area became more and more crime-ridden, Harry and Ruby had been urging her to do, and found a place in town to be closer to them. She lived up the road from Harry and Gwennie's first home, in a low-rooved house originally built for railway workers, in a row of almost identical low-rooved houses, and kept her tiny garden so perfectly neat and manicured, people walking up and down the street would pause to stare over the small, rusty gate at her latest garden ornament or rockery.

Harry would often visit on the weekends, pushing Calvin in his stroller while Gwennie napped. He would almost always find his mother working in her garden, a bright yellow floppy hat pulled down low on her head. The first thing she would do was run her hands under the garden tap, dry them on the sides of her dress and then reach into the stroller for Calvin and hold him tightly to her chest. No matter how niggly he'd been moments before, he was always perfectly at peace in her arms. Harry would roll his eyes and laugh, recounting how many hours it usually took him to get Calvin to be quiet and stop crying, and laughing that she was a walking, talking human baby sedative – and they'd sit on her hot little tin-rooved veranda and talk.

She'd sensed his restlessness even then, his unease about marrying Gwennie, but never interfered, never passed judgement. There was a baby coming, there was no discussion necessary. Neither did she complain when Gwennie openly snubbed her, preferring to leave Calvin with her mother than let Leila babysit him. Harry winced when he thought back to those days, collecting Calvin from his mother-in-law and having to push his way through a new crowd of strangers spilling out of her cramped lounge and onto the veranda. And the smell of alcohol on her breath when she handed him the baby.

Don't fret, son, Leila would tell him as they sat on the veranda, Calvin sleeping on her lap. There's no point. Everything will turn out just as it should, in the end. Harry knew they were precious times, but he had no idea just how precious.

Leila died of a stroke a week after Calvin turned two, and a month before Bernice was born. She very likely died peacefully in her sleep, the doctor assured him, and isn't that the best we can hope for, for those we love?

Harry remembered feeling unreasonably angry with the doctor. No, the best we could hope for was that they could stay with us, that they could grow old with us. That they could see their grandchildren grow. He'd gone home and Gwennie had cooked him his favourite dinner of oxtail and rice and given him one of her stiff, hurried hugs. But the next day it was back to business as usual.

Sometimes he was grateful Leila hadn't been alive to see all that would happen later. He didn't know how she would have coped with finding out about his relationship with Margot, her death and him being sent to jail. He knew she would have fallen apart to see what became of him during that time, and for all those years afterwards.

It will all be OK in the end. Harry couldn't get his mother's words out of his head, even as he sat, too blocked with emotion to cry, at the funeral, a tiny gathering at the local Catholic church attended by a handful of Christian family and friends sitting on the pews inside and Uncle Mohammed standing just outside the door – over 80 at the time, being supported by his son, Jamal, and openly crying. He could still hear his mother's words as he threw a handful of soil into the grave and heard it rain softly on the lid of the wooden coffin. And he could still hear them now, all these years later, as he thought about Calvin and Natalie.

The still afternoon was interrupted by an urgent hooting at the gate and Harry, sitting on the veranda with Sabrina, picked up his stick and walked up the driveway to see who it was.

He was surprised to see Natalie's red car parked at the gate and, as he approached, she stepped out, holding up her hand in greeting.

"Uncle, I'm so sorry to disturb you, but Tamara's missing and I didn't know where else to go!" she said in a rush.

"Natalie, my dear, what happened? When last did you see her?" Harry opened the gate and walked towards her.

"Her dad came over and we got into a fight," she put her hand instinctively to her belly. "He started yelling at me about being an unfit mother and started threatening to go to court and sue for custody! It was awful and I thought at one point he was going to hit me," said Natalie, her voice shaky.

"What brought all this on, my girl?" asked Harry.

"Sorry, Uncle, but he was talking badly about Calvin, saying he wouldn't stand by and see his daughter in the company of someone like that. I told him that Calvin and I aren't together anymore, and besides since when was he so interested in his daughter when he was hardly ever around. But then I regretted the outburst, realising Tam had probably heard every word. I walked out the room, leaving him to rant, and went looking for her but she was nowhere to be seen. I checked with the neighbours, with her best friend's mother, I drove up and down the street calling for her, but I couldn't find her anywhere."

"What can we do to help, girl?"

"Tam grew very attached to Calvin while we were together, and took our break-up hard. She talks about him all the time and when we argue, or when I ask her to do something she doesn't want to do, she says she's going to come live with Calvin, he doesn't shout and he'll look after her." Natalie smiled sadly. "I thought maybe he'd have some idea where to look, or that maybe she'd be trying to make her way here. I just don't know anymore, I'm out of ideas and I'm desperate!"

"I had no idea she was so close to him…" Harry was slowly shaking his head. "Let's call Calvin and see if he knows anything."

He saw her stiffen and then nod lightly. "Please do, Uncle, thank you."

"Would you like to drive the car in?"

"No, thank you. If you don't mind, I'll wait here."

Harry took the slow, long walk to Calvin's apartment at the back and knocked on the door.

"Yo."

"Calvin, I need to see you," Harry called through the door.

There was a fumbling inside and then Calvin opened the door, shrugging on a shirt. He looked down at his father, "Wat's up?"

"Natalie's here, Tamara's missing, she wondered if you knew anything."

"What the fuck?" his brow furrowed.

"Natalie and Tamara's dad got into an argument in front of Tamara and now she's run away. Natalie seems to think Tamara is quite attached to you and may have made her way here – or be trying to."

"Here? What the fuck?" he asked again. Then he disappeared into the apartment and came hurrying out carrying a pair of trainers and socks.

Harry followed him up the driveway and by the time he reached the gate, Calvin and Natalie were already talking heatedly.

"If I had the answers to those questions, I wouldn't be here asking for help," Natalie was saying, her voice close to breaking. "The police won't do anything until she's been missing 24 hours so I can't rely on them – you are literally my last resort!"

They both started getting into the car and Natalie stepped out quickly again to wave a hurried goodbye to Harry. "Thank you, Uncle, please call if you hear anything, and we'll do the same."

He waved back and watched the little red car reverse out of the driveway, on to the road and out of sight.

CHAPTER THIRTY-TWO

THE SILENCE IN the car was palpable. It was the first time they'd seen each other since the fight in the Club and Natalie was aware of the way Calvin had glanced at her loose-fitting dress, the characteristic furrowing of his brows. She was grateful they weren't speaking, weren't trying to talk things through or, worse still, make small talk.

As they drew nearer to her house Calvin asked: "Did you try the Smiths? Ya know how she smaaks to go round and play with their puppies."

"They were the first place I tried." Natalie was holding on tightly to the steering wheel and leaning slightly forward.

"And the Willams?"

"She's always been a little scared of Mr. Williams, she'd never go there alone."

"Why?"

"I know it's silly, but she says he reminds her of the Gruffalo."

Calvin let out a short laugh. "That dinosaur-monster ouen she makes me read to her 10 times a day? I can check how she'd think that!"

Natalie was surprised by the gentleness of his tone.

"Yup, that's the one."

"But the Gruffalo turned out to be a cool ouen."

"The gruff looking ones often do," said Natalie with a little smile. "But would you like to meet him when you're lost and alone and away from home?" And her voice caught in her throat.

"Sut." Calvin sat up straighter in his seat and they both slipped back into silence.

They'd driven up and down each road criss-crossing Natalie's house, and stopped all along the way asking the vegetable vendors if they'd seen her; from their vantage point on strategic street corners, they knew everything that went on in the neighbourhood.

"She's wearing a Lion King T-shirt and she may or may not be wearing pink crocs that light up – those are her favourites but I can't remember if she was wearing them today or not." Natalie closed her eyes and put her palm to her forehead. "Why can't I remember?" And she turned to Calvin.

He was looking intently up and down the road and didn't reply.

They walked back to the car and Calvin looked at her over the roof. "Let's jol to the bottle store. There some ouens I wanna praat to."

The bottle store was at the end of a dingy row of squat-shaped shops; once nicely painted and maintained, today they were the colour of plaster.

With no parking spaces, customers parked their cars outside the shops, often taking up much of the road and forcing other cars to drive around them. There was always at least one car parked directly outside the bottle store, doors and boot open and music pumping. Being a Saturday there were two, each competing to see whose sound system was louder.

People lounged on the chipped steps leading up to the door, drinking, talking and laughing, and when Calvin directed Natalie to park just off the road and stepped out of the car, he was greeted with enthusiastic calls.

Natalie watched as he walked up the steps, shaking hands and pumping fists with people on either side of him. When a woman in a tiny pair of shorts, a halter neck top and too-high heels stood up and tried to hug him and he gently held her at arm's length, Natalie couldn't help but smile.

Finally, he reached the top of the stairs and a scrawny teenager in a string vest and baggy shorts down to his knees jumped up, and he and Calvin shook hands then hugged in the customary way, locked hands crossed in front of their chests and two light taps of their fists to the other's shoulder. Natalie couldn't see his face under his baseball cap, pulled down low on his face, but could see from the way he was standing and leaning towards Calvin, head cocked and arms crossed over his chest, that he was listening intently.

Natalie saw Calvin lean forward, and the teenager start to gesticulate. Calvin reached for his chest and grabbed his vest, then brought him in close to look him in the eye. More gesticulating and Natalie could hear the raised voices but not what was being said.

Calvin gave him a light shove and let go, flicking his hand like he was disposing of a pesky insect, and the teenager stumbled backwards, reaching for the step behind him to steady himself. Calvin turned his back on him and started walking back down the steps, leaving the teenager wildly waving his arms, two of his friends on either side also gesticulating and shouting, but none of them making any attempt to follow.

He stormed back to the car and threw open the door.

"Do they know anything? Have they seen her?"

"Let's get the fuck out of here."

Natalie started the engine and pulled away from the curb and on to the road, and only now did the three youths make a feeble attempt to follow, jogging after them, shouting, and one picking up a stone and flinging it half-heartedly at the retreating car.

"Fuckin' assholes," said Calvin through gritted teeth.

"What happened, what did they say?" Natalie's voice was flimsy with panic.

"They aksed for sheets. Said they'd only tune me the wat-wat if I gave them sheets."

"So they know something?" she looked over at him, her eyes wide.

"Those losers don't know shit, they just after sheets." But there was no disguising the uncertainty in his voice. Natalie could feel her despair gathering like the darkness of the streets they kept driving.

CHAPTER THIRTY-THREE

Sharifa 1954

I DIDN'T KNOW how to tell Marriyam about the visit of her in-laws, my dear Rudo, but after the books were burnt, I felt I had no choice. It all felt too close together, too connected, and I was afraid. For her and for us all.

Her beautiful brown eyes held mine as I recounted the visit, sparing her the lurid details but making it clear what they had come to say. I saw every emotion pass through them as I spoke: shock, anger, fear, but what settled was sadness.

"They burnt the books," she said quietly when I finished.

"We don't know that." I shook my head, not wanting to believe it.

"It's too much of a coincidence."

"Do you think they're capable of such malice?"

"They feel shamed, and want justice – by whatever means."

There she was again, sounding so much older and wiser than her young years.

"The shame is of their own doing."

"Perhaps." Was all she said.

The next few days she was quiet and withdrawn. She'd come home in the evenings and skip dinner, saying she was too tired to eat and retiring early to bed. I tried to bring her out of herself, encourage her to talk, but she was an independent young woman and I couldn't tell her what to do. I felt helpless as I watched her grow drawn and anxious.

Two days later I came home from the soup kitchen around 3 o'clock, as usual, and to my surprise found Marriyam at home cooking over the wood stove.

"My girl, you're home early, is everything OK?"

She smiled a tight smile.

"The cobbler let me go."

"What? But they were so happy with your work, what happened?" I removed my scarf and hung it over the chair and walked over to look at her closely.

"They wouldn't say why, but I know."

I knew too. I had caught the looks of the older women at the Mosque, had heard the whispers. I could see just how it would have happened: the cobbler's wife repeating the rumours to her husband. Her husband not really caring about "women's gossip" and calling her foolish, telling her to keep her nose out of the business. The wife hearing more and more talk, and being gently threatened by the in-laws as I had been. Caring more about her reputation and standing in the community than I did. Maybe having more to lose than I did. Going back and insisting to her husband that "the girl is bad luck, she's been possessed by a jinn, look how business has fallen since she joined us." The cobbler brushing away her protests, calling it nonsense, showing her his workshop, full of orders. But, finally, tiring of her nagging and insistence and agreeing to get rid of Marriyam.

"Oh my girl." I cried that night, I couldn't help myself. And she, that beautiful, brave girl, held me and comforted me and told me not to cry. But the next day she hardly left her room and didn't eat a thing.

I finally drew her out a few evenings later by asking her to bring out her crystals. I knew they always calmed her, and before long we were sitting across from each other at the small table, as we did so often, a hot cup of tea at our sides. I picked out an aquamarine – she'd told me it induced calm – and handed it to her. She rolled it gently back and forth in the palm of her hand and then looked up at me and smiled.

"You've come to know the crystals, and me, so well, Auntie. I want you to have these crystals one day. When I'm no longer around."

"Nonsense!" I tried to keep my tone light, but her words chilled me. "You'll be around a lot longer than me, my girl. Look at me, an old widow with grey hair. Whereas you, you, my darling Marriyam, you have your whole life to live."

"Sometimes, Auntie, I think I may have already seen the best of it. As a little girl growing up, so wild and free. I would play all day long in the streets with my brothers and no one questioned it. I beat the boys at running, at climbing, even at maths." Her eyes sparkled. "Then one day when I was running out the back door with my older brother, Hassan, my mother caught me by the arm and pulled me back in. Not today, girl. Today you'll go upstairs and wash your hands and your face and put on this shalwar kameez I've chosen for you. And you'll behave like a young woman for a change.

"That was the day I met my future husband, promised to him the day I turned 16. I was 13 at the time and he was 15, a spoilt, sullen teenager with bad acne and greasy hair. I had no idea who he was or what he was doing there. If he knew, no one had lectured him about looking and acting properly. About putting on a good show. About behaving. I suppose I was pretty sulky too. I couldn't stop looking out the window, it was such a beautiful Cape day, and all I wanted in the world was to be out there on the street with my brothers, challenging them to a race and feeling the wind in my face as I ran – and the butterflies in my chest when I finished first." Marriyam had closed her eyes, reliving the scene in her mind, a smile on her face.

"Instead I was stuck indoors, glowering at a pimply faced boy, in the midst of a courtship – and I didn't even know it."

She let out a sad, little laugh, staring at the aquamarine in her hand.

We talked late into the night. We talked with the ease of before. We forgot, for a little while, about childhood courtships and pimply boys and the scuffed, dusty brogues of my groom at our Nikkah.

We remembered a time when none of that mattered, when we were just girls with our whole lives ahead of us.

I hugged her extra tight that night. Then I held her at arm's length and looked her in the eyes.

"Never forget how it felt, my girl, the feeling of the wind in your face when you ran. And find that feeling again in your life, it's out there somewhere."

She looked up at me and there were tears in her eyes.

"Tell me you'll never forget." I cupped her face with my hands.

She nodded. A tiny nod, but a nod all the same. I tipped her towards me and kissed her on the forehead. And afterwards she turned away from me all too quickly and I was sure it was so I wouldn't see her cry.

I went to sleep that night uttering a du'a for protection, "In the name of Allah, with whose name there is protection from every kind of harm in the earth and in the heaven, and He is the all-hearing and the all-knowing," my hand clutching the moonstone under my pillow, and finally, some time late in the night, I fell into an uneasy sleep. I was awake again long before dawn and something made me get up and walk through the house. Perhaps I'd heard Marriyam moving around and that was what had made me stir. I wasn't sure. But something had unsettled me. I walked past her room and the door, which had been closed when we'd gone to bed, was open. I called out softly to her.

When there was no answer, I called out a little louder. When still none came, I went inside. But she wasn't in her room, nor was she anywhere in the house. I pressed my face to the window that looked out onto our narrow, cobbled street and squinted through the steam made by my breath on the pane. I wiped it away with the sleeve of my night shirt and looked again through the droplets of condensation so the reflection of my face in the glass seemed to be running with tears. The sky was thick and gloomy, the night's last push before the dawn. I heard the muezzin's dawn call to fajr come tumbling down from the top of the hill and my heart began to pound in my chest, imagining Marriyam out there in the dark. And I began to cry for real.

CHAPTER THIRTY-FOUR

2015

"I NEED YOU to not freak out," Natalie glanced over at Calvin and saw the set of his jaw in alternating light and shadow as they drove under the street lights.

"Freak out about what?" her voice was tight and already beginning to sound shrill.

"I said not to freak out," and he put out his hand as caution and took a deep breath. "Those assholes said something about seeing Tam with a homeless ouen who hangs around the hood, you may have seen him, he always wears black and carries a little charred tin on a chain with coal or somethin' in it, coz there's always smoke coming out of it."

Natalie slammed on brakes and swerved on to the side of the road.

She put the car in park and turned to Calvin. "They've seen her with him, the guy they call Mad Max? Calvin, please tell me it's not true, please tell me you don't believe them!"

"I don't know what to believe, Nat, I'm only tuning you what the ouens told me." And he put up his hands defensively. "But what I do know is that he isn't so much mad," and he put his two fingers to the side of his head like a gun, "as insane – OK, I realise that doesn't help, but ouens tune he's really smart, a genius even, who couldn't deal with the everyday stuff and seeing as no one could understand him he went insane."

Natalie closed her eyes and shook her head as if to erase the image of Mad Max with his little burning pot, long, black dirty cloak trailing the floor and Tamara in tow.

"Did they say what he was doing with her? Where they were? Calvin, I don't know what to do, I am so, so frightened!" She covered her face with her hands and shook her head.

"Jah." Was all Calvin said. And for once he allowed himself to look exactly as lost as he felt.

CHAPTER THIRTY-FIVE

1933

SHARIFA WAITED IMPATIENTLY till first light, and then ran next door and pounded on Auntie Yasmin and Uncle Sameer's house.

Uncle Sameer came to the door in a gown and slippers, looking bleary eyed and worried.

"Sharifa, what is it? Is everything OK?"

"No, Uncle, I'm worried about Marriyam. She left the house long before dawn this morning and with everything that's been happening with her in-laws – did Auntie Yasmin tell you?"

"She did. Those Ayoobs have always been trouble, bullies and crazy people, the lot of them! Too much in-breeding if you ask me, but Auntie Yasmin tells me not to say such things." And his face darkened.

"Well with everything happening, I'm worried for her."

"Come inside, Auntie Yasmin is just finishing her prayers and will come through just now. I'll change and go and try to find out if anyone has seen her."

Uncle Sameer came home close to lunch time. He'd been walking the streets for almost six hours, asking everyone he met if they'd seen Marriyam or knew where she may be.

He walked through the door and slumped, exhausted, into a chair in the kitchen.

"She's gone back." His voice was weary.

"Gone back where?"

"To her husband."

"No! She can't have! It's not true!"

"It is my dear Sharifa."

"Why? Why would she go back? I don't understand!"

"It's not always easy for us to understand, to see things from other people's perspectives."

"But he beat her!"

"He was still beating her – in other ways. Making sure she would never be free. This is a small community, and there is no running away."

"But I would have protected her!"

"How could you, my love?" Auntie Yasmin had come over and put her arms around her. "No amount of good intentions or love could have helped her. She probably saw this as the only way."

"She was protecting you too," added Uncle Sameer. And Sharifa saw her Uncle's eyes were misty with tears. "They weren't going to give up. Only Allah knows what they would have tried next."

But she had to see for herself. She went the next day to Marriyam's in-laws and knocked at the door.

The younger Mrs. Ayoob opened the door. "Yes?" she frowned.

"I'd like to see Marriyam."

The door was closed and she heard voices on the other side. After a long wait the door was opened again, this time by Marriyam, but Sharifa could see the dark bulk of the two Ayoobs just beyond the entrance.

"Auntie," she smiled, but it didn't reach her eyes.

"How are you, my girl?"

"I'm fine, Auntie," she nodded vehemently.

"You left without saying goodbye."

"I'm sorry, Auntie, I didn't want to wake you."

Sharifa lowered her voice. "Is this really what you want?"

Marriyam wouldn't meet her eyes.

"There's no other way."

"Yes, there is, I can help you."

"It's the only way," she whispered. She looked back at Sharifa and their eyes held for the longest time. Then Marriyam broke the silence. "I have to go, it's almost lunchtime and I still have to do the rotis."

Sharifa reached out her arms and Marriyam took a step towards her and the older woman held her close.

Then Marriyam gently pulled away.

"Thank you," she whispered. "I will never forget you. Goodbye."

"Don't talk like you'll never see me again," said Sharifa, reaching out and gently placing a hand on Marriyam's forearm as if to hold on to her a little longer, "I'm just up the road." Sharifa made it sound light, but was begging her with her eyes.

"Good bye," she said again and stepped back and closed the door.

Sharifa was surprised how much she missed Marriyam, and how lonely she felt after she left. It was an unfamiliar feeling. When Khaled had died, she'd relished the solitude. But now the house felt quiet and empty.

During the day she threw herself into her chores, working in the literacy classes after she'd finished at the soup kitchen and getting home just before dark. She thought if she kept busy and wore herself out, she may have no time for thinking. But she'd still find herself lying wide awake, clutching the moonstone but unable to sleep. How was Marriyam? Were they treating her any better than before? The thoughts circled round and round in her head until, a few hours before dawn, she'd fall into a light and restless sleep. And start the cycle all over again.

It was Hassan, Marriyam's older brother, who came to tell Sharifa the news. She'd never met him but when she opened the door, and even before he introduced himself, she saw the same honeyed eyes and the same statuesque build, and knew this must be Marriyam's brother.

"Auntie…," and his voice caught, she thought at first, by embarrassment. Until she looked into his eyes and saw the barely concealed emotion.

She felt panic bubble in her chest.

"What is it? Has something happened? Is Marriyam OK?"

"You were a great friend to my sister, and she wanted me to tell you she loved you very much, that she was grateful for all you did for her, and that she wanted you to have these."

He thrust the bag at her and Sharifa took it but couldn't trust her voice to speak.

She took the bag from him and looked inside. It was Marriyam's wooden box of crystals.

"I don't understand," she finally managed. "Marriyam would never part with her crystals." Her voice was shaky and she dared herself to look up at him.

"My sister's gone," said Hassan, looking down at his shoes.

"Gone? What do you mean gone? Please explain, I don't understand and I am afraid," Sharifa's voice was rising with panic.

"He promised to change, he promised it would be different. The last time he beat her and I came, as her older brother, to speak to him. I tried to reason with my parents to take her in, I really tried. But they were stubbornly stuck on tradition. The shame of her coming home. Now, now we are all soaked in shame."

"Hassan, please tell me what happened! Where is Marriyam?" she had grabbed his arm and started shaking it.

"You know, my sister was the best runner in her year at school? You know she could answer maths questions faster than any boy in my class, and I'm three years older than her. She was so beautiful, my beautiful sister." And now he collapsed on the ground and began to sob.

Sharifa knelt down in the dirt in front of him and took his hand. "Hassan, Hassan, tell me what happened, please, tell me!" she begged him.

"Marriyam is dead."

CHAPTER THIRTY-SIX

2015

IT WAS ALMOST dark when Calvin and Natalie arrived back at the bottle store.

They'd sat side-by-side in the car not saying a word for the longest time, each trying to work out in their minds what to do next.

Natalie was the first to speak. "We have to pay them the money they're asking for," she finally said, looking straight ahead over the steering wheel and on to the increasingly dark road.

"Wat?" Calvin turned to her and frowned.

"They're our only hope right now. It's getting later and we have to find her." Her voice was steady, almost chillingly so.

Calvin sighed.

"OK, it's your sheets, just don't go mal when you find out they were lying to us."

"It's a chance I'm willing to take."

They drove back to the bottle store and as Calvin stepped out of the car Natalie saw him take a deep breath and square his shoulders before slamming the car door and walking towards the steps.

She knew how hard it was for him to come back here after his earlier stand-off and admit that he needed their help. And she realised with a start that Tamara was one of the few people in the world Calvin would squander his street cred for.

Although the group sitting on the steps had thinned, the stringy youth in the vest was still there and Natalie watched him leap to his feet, legs apart and hands bunched into fists at his sides. His chin was cocked, staring down at Calvin from under his cap. He had a cigarette dangling out of the corner of his mouth and Natalie couldn't see the expression on his face through the smoke.

She pulled down her window and heard him shout, "Wat up, dog? So I scheme yous come snivelling back with your tail between your legs?"

Calvin seemed poised to leap at him and then Natalie saw him visibly stop and contain himself. He folded his arms across his chest, she was sure, to stop herself from hitting someone, and spoke in low, steady tones.

After a lengthy exchange, she saw Calvin reach into the pocket of his jeans and take out the roll of money she'd given him. The youth took it from him, the cigarette still dangling from the corner of his mouth, and counted it. Then he shook his head slightly and put out his hand.

Again, she saw Calvin bristle and then control himself. He reached into his pocket and took out another roll, handed it to the youth and then threw up his hands as if to say that was it, there was no more.

The youth painstakingly counted it again, and each

minute seemed to Natalie like a lifetime. He was deliberately stalling.

He shoved the money into the pocket of his shorts and Natalie saw him indicating an overgrown area behind the store. He pointed again and Calvin nodded thoughtfully. Then, as if to declare the discussion over, the youth turned his back on Calvin and started talking to one of his cronies.

Calvin gathered himself together again, ignoring the slight, and trotted back down the steps to the car.

"Fuckin' assholes," he said, ducking his head and folding his body into the seat of the car. "Their time will jol, ya'll see. I have a long memory, especially for assholes."

"What did they say? Did they tell you anything?"

"Jah. She's with him alright. Asshole schemes they headed in that direction about 3 o'clock," he pointed ahead.

"That was over five hours ago!"

"Jah." Calvin nodded his head, suddenly looking exhausted. "Then we'd better jol."

Natalie started up the engine and made to drive in the direction Calvin had indicated. But he reached out and put his hand gently on her arm and said, quite softly, "Jol that way," and he pointed the other way.

"But he said…"

"I know. But ya just gonna have to trust me on this one. I got a feeling I can't shake."

Natalie turned the car around and they started to drive again, both avoiding the stares of the group on the steps as they drove past in the opposite direction.

CHAPTER THIRTY-SEVEN

1933

AUNTIE YASMIN FOUND them like that, both kneeling in the dirt on the street outside Sharifa's house, both crying. She had heard the news at the general dealers and had run to Sharifa to gently break the news to her.

She dropped immediately to the ground beside her and took her niece in her arms, and stroked her hair and spoke soothingly to her, as she had done since she was a little girl.

And then she started to murmur a du'a under her breath, whispering it into Sharifa's ear, to calm herself as much as Sharifa, and slowly Sharifa's sobs abated and she lay her head, exhausted and defeated, on Auntie Yasmin's shoulder, her small shoulders shaking but no sound coming out.

Auntie Yasmin finally managed to persuade Sharifa to get up, helping her to her feet and holding her arm as she walked her into the house; she sat her at the kitchen table and lit the wood stove to make a cup of tea. Sharifa, exhausted by emotion, sat unmoving at the table, her eyes lifeless.

"What happened?" Sharifa finally managed, cupping her hands around the cup of hot, sweet tea Auntie Yasmin made for her.

"They say they fought over the dinner. He shouted at her about the rotis. It wasn't uncommon, he was always shouting, raising his hand to her – as we know, my girl. But this time she spoke back to him. He hit her hard across the face and she fell backwards, hitting her head on the corner of the table as she fell. She was injured but they refused to call a doctor, the aunties saying she would be fine after some rest.

"But, my darling girl, it wasn't the fall that killed her." Auntie Yasmin dropped her eyes, unable to see the pain of what she would say next reflected in her niece's eyes.

"What was it, then, Auntie?" Sharifa put down her cup of tea.

"She drank poison."

Sharifa shrieked, covering her face with her hands.

"Sharifa, my darling Sharifa," said Auntie Yasmin, taking her in her arms again. "We have to believe she is at peace now, we have to believe this was the only way she thought she could be free."

"But it wasn't! That's the tragedy! It wasn't."

She cried for a long time, Auntie Yasmin holding her tight and whispering soothingly to her.

"Who told you?" Sharifa finally managed.

"Hassan. He refuses to remain silent any longer and has reported them to the Imam. He saw her after the fall, insisted on seeing her. She was stoic, he said, but somehow defeated. He says he wishes he had done something then. He blames himself. There are good people out there, my darling girl, and they will make sure justice is served," she pulled slightly away to look Sharifa in the eyes.

"What justice, Auntie? What good people? If they were good people, Marriyam would still be alive! May they all rot in Jahannam!"

"Don't say that, my sweet girl, don't let them break your beautiful spirit."

"They have already broken my heart, what else is there?"

Sharifa would not be consoled. Auntie Yasmin begged her to come to their house for the night but she refused and, instead, Auntie Yasmin persuaded her to go to bed and try to get to sleep, and after consulting with Uncle Sameer, made a bed in Marriyam's old room and slept there to be near her niece.

She lay awake all night listening to Sharifa pacing her room, and her own pounding heart, filled with fear for what lay ahead and unable to shake the feeling that none of them would ever be the same again.

Sharifa 1954

I don't remember how many days I took to my bed after Marriyam died, dear Rudo. The days seemed to blur one into the other. I remember Auntie Yasmin, that beloved woman, coming into my room with food, with drink, with sweet words, with tears running down her face imploring me to eat. But I could not.

But finally I found the strength to get out of bed, to wash for the first time in days, and to try to eat something. When Auntie Yasmin came through late that morning, having prepared Uncle Sameer's lunch before coming back to check on me, she saw me sitting at the kitchen table and squealed with happiness and relief, and it pained me to think how much anxiety I had caused her.

I started apologising to her for it, and she, in her usual way, brushed it all away.

You are my daughter and your pain is my pain, your joy is my joy too.

I convinced her I would be OK and urged her to go back to her own house, her own bed, back to Uncle Sameer who had been so patient and generous, allowing her to dedicate herself the last days to my well being.

She left reluctantly, but not before bringing me a pot full of her famous chicken biriyani and a dozen freshly made rotis.

My sweet mother, I remember looking at her with love, how do you imagine I'll eat 12 rotis on my own? You need to get your strength back, my girl, and I know you won't disappoint your aunt by letting them go to waste.

She kissed me on the forehead and left, and as soon as she pulled the door shut behind her I went to my room and retrieved the bag Hassan had given me with Marriyam's box of crystals. Somehow, through the pain and the grief of the last few days, the thought that the box was lying near me, though I didn't have the courage to open it, had sustained me.

Now I opened the box for salvation and for release, and that was when I found the note. Marriyam had worked on her writing every day since she'd come to live with me and the letters, although shaky, were clearly legible.

Do not be sad. I can feel the wind in my face again. I am free. I love you.

I read the note over and over, willing myself to hear her voice, to see her sweet smile, feel her hand in mine. I folded the note and put it under my pillow, next to my moonstone, then reached into the box and took out the amethyst. The amethyst brings peace, I heard her tell me, looking at me with those beautiful honey eyes as we sat at the kitchen table one evening soon after she moved in.

It calms the mind, calling on our own infinite wisdom deep inside us and bringing us back to spirituality where all peace lies. Her eyes grew even brighter.

I found a piece of muslin then, and cut it into a square. I placed the amethyst in the centre and slowly stitched it together making a little pouch. Then I braided strands of thread together to form a bracelet and threaded the pouch through. I fastened it around my wrist and pulled down the sleeve of my kameez to cover it. Be at peace, my precious girl, I whispered, before closing my eyes, raising my palms and saying a du'a for protection.

I turn to Rudo in the half light of dawn all these years later. Her eyes are on me, wide with wonder and bright with tears as she listens to my story. I pull up my sleeve and show her. I still wear it today. For Marriyam. For my beloved Auntie Yasmin and Uncle Sameer, may Allah rest their dear souls, for Ali, for you and dear Leila and my darling Harry and Rudo. After all that our family has witnessed and endured for so many years, it's all I really ask for. Peace.

"Shariah law clearly prescribes ta'zir for the man who uses such force on a wife that it leads to her injury or death," said Uncle Ibrahim, incessantly fiddling with his prayer beads.

"So what punishment will he receive?" Hassan asked.

"Marriyam did not die as a result of her husband's blow –

or any blow. The family insists she was not in any way hurt. We know, of course, that they would not freely admit it, but we only have their word against yours."

"I saw the marks, everyone did!"

"When?"

"All the time."

"When was the last time, son?"

"Two days before she died."

"And when you saw her two days before she died, did you think her injuries severe enough to cause her death? And remember, honesty is of utmost importance."

"But it was clear what he was doing to her."

"Son, that is not the question."

Hassan sighed heavily. "No."

"Was she alert, conscious, did she speak to you clearly?"

"Yes." And Hassan hung his head.

"And that, son, is our first dilemma. Our second is that Marriyam took her own life. Of that we have the testimony of the respected Moslem doctor who attended to her and who issued the death certificate. There was a note to her family, was there not?"

"Yes." Hassan kept his eyes on the ground.

"As we know, the act of suicide is a sin in the eyes of Allah."

"Beating your wife is a sin!" Hassan looked up, his eyes alight with rage.

"Yes, my son, it is. But my hands are tied."

Hassan's hands were shaking right up to the point when he knocked on the door. When it was opened by the younger aunt, he was suddenly perfectly calm.

"Auntie, I have come to see Nabil on behalf of my family, to make amends."

She hmphed but went back inside and called Nabil.

Hassan didn't wait to see his expression or hear him open his mouth in greeting, but calmly, steadily, took a step forward and opened his arms as if to hug his brother-in-law. And when Nabil took a step towards him, somewhat confused, Hassan embraced him with one arm and with the other pulled a knife out of his pocket and thrust it upwards, into his heart. Then he stepped back.

Too shocked to even cry out, Nabil looked down at the blade, still inside him, then up at Hassan. Then down at the blade and again at Hassan. He reached for it and feebly tried to remove it, but he was weak with shock and rapidly losing blood. Hassan didn't move, didn't say a word. And when the aunties ran, shrieking, to their bleeding nephew's side, he still didn't move. When Nabil dropped to his knees and then collapsed forward, he still remained motionless. And then, when he was sure he could not be resuscitated, he walked calmly to Imam Ibrahim, Nabil's blood still on his hands, and knelt at his feet.

"Suicide is a sin, and so is murder. I am ready to join my sister in Janna or Jahannam, wherever Allah deems we belong. As long as he allows us to be together."

Imam Ibrahim was not an emotional man. He had had to make too many hard decisions in his life, had had to uphold the word of Allah to the last letter at every cost, without giving in to sentimentality. But the day he watched Hassan being handcuffed and thrown into a police carriage to serve out his life imprisonment, the old man went home, retreated to his room and closed the door. Then he leant his back against it and he cried. He cried so hard his thick white beard became saturated and, much later, when his wife came knocking tentatively at the door to call him to dinner, he asked her to please leave him be, he was tired and unwell and would not eat dinner that night.

Sharifa 1954

If I could, I would have left the Cape the day Marriyam died. I wanted to get as far away as possible from the pain and the memories. But Uncle Sameer fell ill that year, soon followed by Auntie Yasmin. They were both in their 80s by then. And I dedicated those next years to caring for them as they had done for me my whole life. They died in the same year, Auntie Yasmin first, quietly in her sleep, and Uncle Sameer, bereft of the love of his life, two months later. I was heartbroken, but so grateful I could be by their sides and serve them in this small way. There seemed no other reason to stay after that, especially as there were already rumbles about the Group Areas Act and the threat which hung over our heads that the Malay Quarters would be relocated like District Six had been. No one felt at ease, the tension and anxiety were terrible. I was ready to come at last to Rhodesia. But there was another motivation too: Marriyam's death, while shaking me to my very core, made me determined to live my life with purpose, to live as honestly as I could. To be free, as she had always longed to be free. And I couldn't do that while still carrying the secrets of my past. I had no means to come then, and my heart ached every day with longing. And then my beloved Ali died and it seemed like my world had fallen apart again. Still, I knew I must come. When Uncle Sameer and Auntie Yasmin's estate was finally settled, many years later, I was left part of the inheritance, not much but enough to buy me passage here. All these years later I followed Ali and Mohammed, all the time imagining my two sweet boys, so young and so innocent, leaving me and everything they knew to travel across these vast seas to an unknown land. And I finally saw my beloved Ali again, reflected in the eyes of my beautiful granddaughter, and in the love he left imprinted on his world.

It was too late for Ali and me, my dear Rudo, but not too late for you and me. I have felt, these last few years, a great spiritual connection to Ali and to Marriyam. I sense them watching over me, guiding me, urging me to be brave. And so I'm ready to leave my story, the whole story, at your feet, in your hands, in your prayers, for I am too old and too tired to carry it alone any longer.

CHAPTER THIRTY-EIGHT

1902

SHARIFA HAD SPENT a miserable night after Evan told her he was going away for good, tossing and turning so much that she eventually went to the kitchen, pulled a chair up to the fireplace and sat staring into the soot and ash.

When she heard the knock on the door the next morning, she ran to it, her heart in her throat. It was Evan, she told herself, coming to tell her he wasn't going, or at least giving her a chance to say a proper goodbye. Winding his way through the cramped little streets of the Malay Quarters to find her house again, like that time he came to drop off money on behalf of his mother when she forgot to pay her, and just in time for her to rush to the general dealer to buy flour for the rotis for that night's dinner.

She'd been so startled then, so embarrassed by her appearance, her dirty apron tied around her waist, yellowed with turmeric, and her hair tousled under the head scarf she'd hastily fastened over it when she heard the knock. But this time, this time she couldn't wait to see him.

She threw the door open and looked straight ahead. But the eyes that met her – though the same startling shade of green – didn't hold any of Evan's warmth or kindness.

Sharifa gasped and stepped back, her hand still on the door frame, and looked down at the floor.

"Surprised to see me?" his voice was as hard as his eyes. "It wasn't easy to find you, Evan refused to tell me, but I am nothing if not resourceful."

She was too startled to speak.

"Aren't you going to invite me in? What, none of the warm welcome you show my brother?" He spread his arms wide. "Or is the warm welcome only for the men you bed?"

"What?" Sharifa's eyes shot up to his, met them and held them. "What are you saying?"

"Oh, don't act coy with me!" He took a step closer and she stepped back.

They were inside the door and Thomas shoved it shut. He took another step towards her and looked her up and down, his gaze lingering on her breasts. "You are beautiful, it's true – if you like that sort of look. But I could have found Evan 20 women as beautiful, if not more so. What is it about you? What is this spell you've woven that is making my little brother defy me? What have you done to make him refuse to take up his rightful responsibilities to his family and stay here to teach school instead!" and he spat. "What is it, witch?" he bellowed, taking another step towards her. Sharifa cowered.

"I don't know what you're talking about. Evan is my friend, Evan helped me. Please get out. Please get out of my home!"

"Helped you? Ha! I'm sure he did. Now why don't you show me how? Why don't you show me just how Evan helped you?"

He lunged forward and took hold of her small wrist, his huge hand completely encircling it.

"Evan told me exactly how you helped him." His voice was low and leaden. "He told me everything. He told me how you lured him here, with your false modesty, your syrupy dreams to read and write. How you persuaded him not to go to the Transvaal! And for what? Where did you think that was going to get you, besides inside my brother's pants?"

"It's not like that, what are you saying? Evan would never say that, please, please let go of my hand, please, you're hurting me. Please!" And she tried to twist and turn out of his grasp but he only held on tighter.

With one hand still wrapped around her wrist he used the other to tear off her head scarf.

Sharifa shrieked and with her free hand covered her face, tried to hide her hair. He flung her hand away and stepped closer, pushed himself against her and pressed his mouth roughly on hers. She was tossing her head from side-to-side, trying desperately to pull away, but was no match for his strength.

"What is it! Aren't I good enough for you? My brother was good enough for you, and I'm twice the man he'll ever be! Here, let me show you!" His hot breath was on her, his lips pulled back, baring his teeth. The shadows of a face she realised in that moment she'd come to love, contorted with contempt.

He pushed her down to the cold stone floor and pressed himself on top of her. Sharifa could hardly breathe, hardly think. And she turned her head away so she wouldn't have to see what hatred could do to those beloved green eyes.

Sharifa 1954

In one frighteningly lucid moment, my darling Rudo, I finally realised I knew what it felt to love. The love my aunties described to me on my Mehndi night. And in the same moment I learnt abject hate. Two opposite emotions clothed in two men, so strikingly similar and yet nothing alike. Two faces of one coin. Sometimes, my dear child, the two emotions are so mixed up, so blended together we can no longer separate one from the other.

When he finally got off me and his weight was lifted from my chest, I thought I would be able to breathe again, but I could not. I wondered if I would ever breathe easily again. I heard the rustle of breeches being pulled up, refastened. I kept my head turned to the side, my eyes closed tight. I lay there on the hard floor long after I heard his boots thud away, the door slam. I rolled over and curled myself into a ball, and I would have stayed like that forever if I could. But the thought of Mohammed, and Khaled coming home soon, forced me to get up.

I was bruised, inside and out. I dragged myself to the basin of water I kept in the kitchen for washing dishes. I scooped up the icy water in my hands and splashed it on my face. I washed my face and hands raw. Then I smoothed down my hair and changed my crumpled clothes. I put my headscarf back on and I somehow walked to Mrs. Lala's to pick up Mohammed, though to be honest, my dear Rudo, I have no recollection of how I got there.

With Mohammed's tiny hand in mine, listening to him chirp away innocently about his day, I slowly felt my mind clear, drag itself to the present. And by the time I served the dinner, my hands had almost stopped shaking.

Khaled was in a particularly foul mood that evening. The dinner was cold, the rotis were hard, the curry was tasteless.

Sharifa let it all go over her head. Her mind was too full to process any of it tonight.

"So? What do you have to say for yourself?" He'd pushed his chair away from the table and was sitting looking at her, his fists planted on the table's edge.

"I'm sorry?" She stopped clearing away the dishes and looked at him.

"I said, what do you have to say about your cooking? I knew when I married you I wasn't getting a woman of wealth or standing, that I was getting a penniless orphan. Beauty, yes, but that fades – doesn't it?" And he looked her over. "I thought the least I could expect was a woman who could cook well and keep a good home. And then I get this." And he flicked his hand dismissively at the table and the dishes on it.

Sharifa took a deep breath and momentarily closed her eyes. "Sorry," she managed through gritted teeth.

"Sorry isn't good enough!" he yelled, throwing back his chair so it clattered onto the floor. He stormed to the door, took his coat off the hook and held it in one hand while pulling down on the door handle with his other. Then he left, slamming the door behind him.

Sharifa's only consolation was knowing that when he eventually came back, he would have found what he needed at the wharf and would leave her alone. At least for tonight.

She looked over at Mohammed, sitting in his little chair turning the pages of a book; and the fact that he no longer became upset and started crying when his father shouted made her sadness deepen even further.

CHAPTER THIRTY-NINE

2015

NATALIE'S HANDS WERE shaking so badly she was having trouble driving.

"Calvin, would you drive?" she asked, turning to him.

"Jah, pull over there," he said indicating a clearing in the bush on the side of the road.

Natalie was grateful Calvin was at the wheel as they navigated increasingly deteriorating roads which, once they left the dim glow of the last row of houses, eventually disintegrated altogether. Although they were driving slowly, the wheels were churning up dust which danced in the headlights and limited their visibility. They were straining their eyes, trying to see beyond the arc of the headlights, but there was no sign of life.

"We gonna have to park up and jol by foot," said Calvin looking across at her. "I don't scheme we'll see anything from the road."

Natalie nodded and he pulled over. They stepped out of the car and he locked it with the remote. They crossed the road towards an area of thick bush and Calvin took out his phone and turned on the flash light, shining it on the ground in front of them. He took her hand and helped her over a gully separating the road from the bush and, afterwards, when she didn't pull her hand away, he kept holding it.

"Tamara!" Natalie began to call, and Calvin squeezed her hand and started to call out too, their calls becoming increasingly louder the further into the bush they crept.

"Calvin, maybe we shouldn't be doing this alone," Natalie stopped and turned to him. "Maybe we should have brought someone along with us."

"Someone like who?"

"I don't know, like a policeman?"

"What the po-po gonna do? They more clueless than anyone."

"But we don't know what we're going to find." And her voice broke.

"Nah, we don't. But we just gotta keep joling. Time ain't on our side."

They kept walking and calling out, the foliage becoming so thick it seemed to snatch their calls straight out of the air and swallow them whole, and Natalie began to wonder if, after this, she'd have any voice left at all – to call, to cry, to say her daughter's name again.

CHAPTER FORTY

1902

SHARIFA FINISHED THE laundry she had collected the previous day and sent Salmaan to deliver it, and to tell all her customers that she had taken ill and would not be able to continue working for them.

Then she shut herself away for the next fortnight, only leaving the house to take Mohammed to school and collect him again at lunchtime. She stopped once or twice at the general dealers, using the money saved up from Evan to buy meagre household supplies, but made sure to hurry in and out without having to talk to anyone.

She made an extra effort with the dinner to avoid Khaled's ire and although he didn't compliment it, he didn't complain either. When he reached for her the first time after it happened, she braced herself and didn't cry out, though she was still bruised and sore. And afterwards she lay staring at the ceiling till long after midnight.

Sharifa started to pray. More than she had ever prayed before. Until that point, her faith had been an intangible force which had formed her childhood and guided her path.

But now it became her salvation. Sharifa prayed day and night to Allah to forgive her, to guide her, to heal her, and the moments of solitude with her creator, day after day, slowly brought her solace and peace.

When after two weeks she was ready to face the world again, she went straight to Auntie Yasmin and asked how she could become more involved in the activities of the Mosque and the Moslem Women's Society.

"My sweet Sharifa," smiled Auntie Yasmin, "I always knew you would come to me when you were ready. Together we are going to do wonderful things for the community and for the glorification of Allah's name, Alhamdulillah!"

When the morning nausea started a month later, Auntie Yasmin smiled gently at her again. "I told you love would grow, my sweet Sharifa. You will see, with the birth of your second child, your happiness will be complete." Sharifa was too sick – and too afraid – to reply, and kept her eyes fixed on her hands, busily sorting dal for the soup kitchen.

CHAPTER FORTY-ONE

1902

SHARIFA WAS TWO months pregnant when she saw Evan again and still not showing under her shalwar kameez. They met at the market, where she went every couple of days, and she couldn't tell if he'd come looking for her, or bumped into her by accident.

She saw him and the shrill sounds of the market sellers and frenzied customers all around her faded away and all she could hear was her heart pounding in her chest.

He seemed to have aged overnight, and there was a hardness at the corners of his mouth which had once creased so easily into a smile.

Her heart began beating so wildly in her chest she thought she may faint, and although she wanted to turn and run away, she found herself rooted to the ground.

She looked down in her customary way when he approached her.

"Sharifa."

"You look like a real businessman," she said softly, aware of the shaking in her voice.

And she heard the sad smile in his voice when he answered, "So cruel?"

"Who would know cruelty better than us?" she replied, still looking down.

She heard him draw in his breath.

"My brother told me about your meeting."

She gasped and looked up, searching his face, but his expression was set.

"I had thought we were friends, that you could have told me yourself that you never wanted to see me again, rather than sending a message through Thomas."

She tried to reply, thought in all honesty didn't know what to say, but he put up a hand to stop her and gently shook his head.

"There's no need to try and explain, Sharifa. I finally put aside my childish ways and I now see the world for what it is. I must apologise for compromising you with my naivete. For inserting myself in your life. It was foolish folly. I could have put you in danger, and I am sorry. I assure you, I will never trouble you again, and wish you all the best in your life."

And before she could say a word, he tipped his hat in her direction and hurried away.

Sharifa lay awake long after Khaled fell asleep, lying on his back and snoring loudly. Hours before dawn she got out of bed and went into the kitchen, then she sat at the table, her head bowed, and started to pray. She begged Allah to take away the agonising sorrow in her heart and in her mind, imploring Him to help her to love the new life inside of her and forgive her sins. Afterwards, she sat with her hand resting lightly on her belly, willing herself to face the day ahead, and when she felt a flutter, so light it could have been mistaken for wind, Sharifa couldn't help but smile. Allah is quick to answer the prayers of those who pray to Him with a pure heart, she heard Auntie Yasmin whisper to her, holding her close the day she told her she was pregnant the first time.

Ali came into the world as he would live his life: loudly. "He has your fair skin," said the midwife satisfactorily before handing him, cleaned and swaddled, to Sharifa, and she bent down to look at a tiny face, scrunched up with indignation at being thrust into the light and noise of this strange new world. She kissed him gently on the forehead and with the help of the midwife, set about getting him to feed.

As was customary, Sharifa and the boys moved in with Auntie Yasmin for the first 40 days of Ali's life. Khaled would visit every evening and often stay for dinner. The first few days he stood awkwardly at the crib peering in, or as Ali lay in Sharifa or Auntie Yasmin's arms. But after a week, and with Auntie Yasmin's encouragement, he took Ali into his arms for the first time. He swayed awkwardly from side-to-side and when Ali opened his eyes and looked at him for the first time, Khaled called out, excitedly: "He has Uncle Rashid's eyes!"

Sharifa's heart was beating in her throat. She had noticed the green flecks in Ali's eyes, almost indistinguishable at first, unless, like her, you were looking for them. But the more alert he became, and the more he opened his eyes, the more distinct they became.

"Uncle Rashid?" she asked in a small voice.

"Yes, my father's uncle, he died long before we married. He had green eyes just like Ali!"

And Sharifa mouthed a silent prayer of thanks.

By the time Ali was two, his eyes were his most distinctive feature, and people commented on them wherever they went. They were so different, her little boys, in nature as well as looks. Mohammed swarthy with big brown eyes, serious and studious, always looking out for his mischievous little brother. Ali, fair like Sharifa, as noisy as his brother was quiet, and with a deep curiosity for the world around him. Ali's easy and uncontrolled laugh both haunted and delighted her.

Around this time, while re-packing her clothes in her drawer, Sharifa came across her long-hidden pencil and paper and a flood of emotions washed over her. She took the pencil in her hand, her long, tapered fingers pressed together close to the nib, and she smiled. Then she took the pencil and paper to the kitchen table and tried to remember what she had learnt. It had been so long ago she found she couldn't remember much, but went to Mohammed's school bag and took out one of his reading books and slowly, methodically, found and wrote each letter of the alphabet as the priest had instructed them.

And then she used the words to form the letters to her son's names. It took her a long time to complete it, working a little at a time, until finally she mastered it. Mohammed and Ali, Ali and Mohammed, over and over again in neat lines across the paper. Until they filled the entire page. Until she had it perfect.

Khaled was quick with his tongue, but he rarely lashed out at her physically. The day he found the paper was one of the few occasions he struck her and, afterwards, Sharifa wondered which was worse. At least her lip would heal with a little ice and ointment. And now people could see. Auntie Yasmin had hugged her extra tight when she'd come over with fresh vegetables from the market that day. Her aunt didn't ask any questions, and Sharifa offered no explanation.

But this time she didn't stop writing, as she had when Evan went away. She just became better at hiding it. A little at a time, every day, after Khaled left for work or in the evenings when he was in bed. Those were her favourite times. Sitting at the kitchen table, the coals from the fire still smouldering, Mohammed's reading book on one side, her paper on the other, copying the words in the warm light of the candle.

Mohammed and Ali. Mohammed and Ali. My sons. I love my sons. Allah love my sons and keep them safe.

CHAPTER FORTY-TWO

1907

SHARIFA SAW EVAN again when Mohammed was 7 and Ali 5. She'd started taking in laundry to help pay the bills, though nowhere near the Godwins which she avoided at all costs. Mohammed was helping her carry the tub and Ali was skipping ahead with a stick, turning around and running reluctantly back whenever he went too far and Sharifa called him. He was running back to her and not looking where he was going when he nearly ran into a man walking with a woman on his arm.

"Steady on," the man laughed good naturedly.

Ali ducked, mumbling an apology, and darted to Sharifa's side. Sharifa had put down the tub and turned to Ali to reprimand him, and didn't see Evan until he was right in front of her.

He was staring at Ali, then at Sharifa, then back to Ali.

"Apologies for my son," she mumbled, her eyes on the ground. Her heart was beating wildly and she was struggling to keep her voice steady. "He never looks where he is going." By this time Mohammed had walked over to his brother and was adding his reprimand to his mother's.

"No matter, no harm done," Evan hesitated and his voice faltered.

Then the woman on his arm tugged gently and they carried on walking. Evan glanced back once; he saw Mohammed struggle to lift the tub on his own, his mother step up and insist they do it together, and Ali, stick in hand, right back to skipping up the street ahead of them without a care in the world.

"So it's true?" said Evan the moment she opened the door to his knock. She hurriedly beckoned him in, looking around to make sure no one had seen him, before closing the door behind them.

"What are you doing here?" she searched his eyes, red and swollen with lack of sleep. Sharifa's hands were visibly shaking.

"I had to see you, I had to know if it's true." He was holding his hat between his hands, fiddling incessantly with the band and looking everywhere but at her.

"What's true? What are you talking about?" she was staring up at him.

"If it's true about you and my brother." And now he looked her straight in the eyes.

"What?" her voice was a whisper.

"When he told me you'd seduced him, I didn't believe him. He swore he didn't know at the time that we were friends. He said you lured him on the pretence of talking to him about me, and then seduced him. All these years, Sharifa. All these years, I thought he was a liar. And now I see your son. Those are Thomas's eyes, Sharifa. I don't understand! Did I really mean so little to you?"

"Evan, Evan please, please believe me, it wasn't like that," and she stretched out her arm to lightly touch his arm but he shrugged her off.

"How was it then?" he threw his hat on the ground and looked at her, his eyes full of tears.

"Oh Evan," Sharifa held her hands close to her chest, twisting them together. "How could you believe that of me?"

"What other explanation is there? I don't understand!" he said again.

"What he did to me, what I have endured. I can not…"

"What do you mean, what are you talking about?" His voice had grown quiet.

"I can not, Evan. He is your brother. I can not. But ask him. Ask him again what happened. What he did to me."

"What are you saying?" Evan bent down to pick up his hat and started fiddling with it again. "If that's true, why didn't you say something? Why didn't you tell anyone, why didn't you tell me?" His eyes were wide and searching.

"Look at me, Evan, look at me! And then look around you! Don't be so naïve. What could I have done? What could I have said? All I can do is thank Allah with every breath in my body that my husband had an uncle with green eyes. That's all I'm reduced to Evan, prayer. Prayer. For forgiveness, for hope, for a better life for my sons. Both my sons."

"But…."

"I think you should leave. You can't be seen here. And I can not look at you without seeing him." And with that she turned her back to him and covered her face with her hands. And she didn't move until long after she heard him walk towards the door, open it and pull it shut behind him.

The most telling part was that Evan believed her so easily. Not only because it was Sharifa. That was one of the things he loved about her – her ability to state, in her quiet, gentle way, the absolute truth. She never skirted it, never ran away from it, had the courage to tell the truth when everyone around her lied. The other reason he believed it was because it was Thomas. Thomas, who treated all women – and most men too – with a disregard that came with power. Evan had closed his eyes when she'd said it, and pictured the time he'd walked in on Thomas and a young servant girl who worked for the family. She couldn't have been more than 14 or 15. Thomas had both her wrists in his hands, pinning them down next to her body; he was leering towards her and she was straining away. Thomas, what's going on, he'd shouted. He was startled and immediately let go of her wrists and dismissed her with a toss of his hand. She ran from the room and the two brothers were left alone. What was that about? Evan was very young, and in awe of Thomas back then – that word awe, with both the elements of wonder and fear that it contains. He didn't question it when Thomas said she'd burnt a hole in the cuff of his new shirt and when he'd reprimanded her, she'd become insolent. She needed to know her place. It niggled Evan, but he did nothing. When their father died, Thomas took over as Evan's guardian and mentor. It was Thomas who schooled Evan on the family business, who forced him to stop teaching and sent him off to the Transvaal to run the family interests there. He'd laugh at Evan's love of books and reading and teaching, and taught his little brother how to shoot a gun instead. A real man needs to know how to shoot, Evan, not read poetry. The only thing poetry is good for is to seduce a woman – but we don't need that, my boy, we're Godwins. We take what we want! And, as he'd said it, he'd grabbed Evan around the shoulders and pulled him close, tousling his hair and laughing. Evan had laughed along with him, though he didn't really know what he meant. What was it to be a Godwin? None of it had ever meant to Evan what it had meant to Thomas.

Now they were both adults and Evan had less of the wonder but still all the fear.

CHAPTER FORTY-THREE

1907

"WE NEED TO talk about Sharifa," Evan stood in the doorway to Thomas's office, his hands clenched into fists at his sides.

"Who?" Thomas was working at his desk and didn't even bother looking up.

But when Evan said it again, louder this time, Thomas looked up from his papers, surprised by his brother's tone.

He took in Evan's red eyes and dishevelled appearance and his mouth tightened at one corner.

"I have no idea who you're talking about."

"You know very well who I'm talking about! Sharifa, my friend, my student at the adult literacy classes! You know exactly who I'm talking about – and what you did to her!" Evan's voice was rising.

Thomas shoved back his chair and it rattled to the ground.

He planted his two massive hands on the desk in front of him and raised himself to his full height, looking down at his little brother from under dark brows.

"Now you listen to me, Evan, and you listen to me good! You will check your tone – and your accusations!" he thundered.

"Or?" Evan lost his courage for a moment, feeling every bit again the scared little boy so easily bullied by his brother. Then the image of Thomas and the servant girl flashed into his mind and he said it again, much louder than before. "Or, Thomas? Or what will you do?"

In one deft move, Thomas leaned across his desk, grabbed Evan's collar and yanked him towards him. His face was inches from Evan's so he could smell his breath, and his voice was deathly low. "Who do you think you are, you fucking little brat? Coming into my home, my office and accusing me of impropriety with one of your whores! That's the whole point of whores, Evan! There is no propriety with whores, that's the beauty of it, wouldn't you agree? Wouldn't you agree?" He screamed into Evan's face, splattering him with fine spittle. "And you'd know that if you weren't such a God-damn child!"

Evan was heaving with emotion. He closed his eyes momentarily, and when he opened them Thomas saw the rage in them, but had no time to react. Evan reached behind Thomas's head and grabbed a handful of hair at the nape of his neck. And he slammed his head into his desk. Thomas yelled, with surprise as well as pain, but Evan didn't let go. Instead, he raised Thomas's head, averting his eyes from the cut on his forehead, already starting to seep blood, and slammed it down a second time.

Thomas howled, and, with his head still held down on the desk, reached behind him and plucked Evan's hand off his neck. Then he threw himself across the desk and on to him and the two men fell to the floor, Thomas crushing his brother with his weight.

Evan matched Thomas in strength and anger and grabbed his shoulders, rolling him over till he was on top of him. Then he gripped Thomas's collar with his left hand and brought his fist down hard on his jowl with his right.

"Say her name!" he screamed.

"Get off me, you fucking ingrate!"

"Say her name, damn you!"

"I don't remember the names of whores!" And Evan punched him a second time.

"Her name is Sharifa. Say her name! Say her name!"

And Evan lost himself, blindly punching Thomas till a man servant, alerted by the noise, ran in and pulled him off.

Thomas leapt to his feet and swung a low and savage blow to Evan's abdomen. Evan was winded, holding his abdomen and stumbling backwards. Thomas took his opportunity and kicked him in the groin, and watched as his brother fell backwards.

He towered over him, blood trickling from the corner of his mouth, and with one last kick to his ribs, muttered "She has no name. She's just another whore. Get him out of here."

Evan was pulled to his feet and helped out the door. He was bent over in agony, hugging his midriff. But the pain in his raw fist, he noted with a warped sense of satisfaction, was even sharper.

CHAPTER FORTY-FOUR

2015

"WHAT'S THAT?" NATALIE stopped and tugged on Calvin's hand.

"What?"

"That glow," she pointed ahead through the bushes.

"I don't see nada," Calvin turned off his flash light and squinted into the darkness.

"Maybe my eyes are playing tricks on me, but I think I see a fire up ahead. Don't you see it?

"Sut." He shook his head, but started to sniff the air, inhaling deeply.

"Do you smell something?"

"Dunno, scheme I may smell smoke, but there's always a span of ouens lighting fires in the bush. I dunno."

He turned his flash light back on, pulled gently on her hand and quickened his step.

She sensed the increased urgency in him and started calling out again. "Tamara! Tamara, honey, where are you? Tamara? It's Mama and Calvin, we've come to find you."

Now she could smell it too, the distinct smell of smoke, not a regular wood fire but rich and peaty like coal.

"Calvin, I smell it too," her voice was thin.

"Jah." He was walking very fast now and she was struggling to keep up but didn't let go of his hand.

"Tamara!" Calvin called. "Tam! Where are you? Anyone out there? Answer us, God-dammit! Who the fuck are you? If you've hurt one hair on that little girl's head I swear to God I'm gonna fuck you up so fuckin' bad!"

Natalie let go of his hand and held on to the crook of his arm, and could feel his muscles trembling with adrenaline.

"What the fuck!" They heard footsteps and a loud rustling and Calvin pulled away and started running in the direction of the sound. Natalie wanted to follow but realised that she wouldn't be able to keep up. She took her phone out of her pocket and shone the flash light through the bushes but all she could see was Calvin's light, flickering through the bushes and then out of sight.

"Calvin!" she yelled after him. "Be careful!"

She could hear panting and grasping, and the rustling in the bushes which seemed to get louder and wane as Calvin and whoever he was chasing threaded in and out of the foliage.

Her heart in her throat, she started running in the same direction.

"Calvin! Calvin!"

The smell of burning coal was growing stronger, pricking at her nose and catching in her throat. But she kept running, pushing her way through the dense bush and oblivious to the branches slicing her hands and bare arms.

She pushed through and into a small clearing and stopped dead in her tracks. A man dressed all in black, so he seemed to be merged with the night, was standing over something lying in a dark heap on the floor and swinging a little black pot over it, smoke rising out of it in thick, dark curls.

CHAPTER FORTY-FIVE

Sharifa 1930

THE LOVE OF a mother for her child is so great, my darling Ali, that it eclipses every other emotion. I used to worry, before you were born, that I would be unable to love you, that I would look at you and remember him. But the genes you shared with my torturer, you also shared with my beloved, and over time I realised, with immense relief, that your green eyes held all of Evan's light and love, and none of his brother's darkness. Over time, my sweet boy, I forced myself to erase that day altogether, and fooled my mind into forgetting. In my mind, you were Evan's child, with his easy laugh and kindly ways, your bright mind and your ceaseless spirit. In my mind you were born of a love that was sweet and whole, the kind of love my aunties told me about, the kind of love I longed for. The love I would take to the grave, along with my secrets. But I've realised, as I've grown older, that I want to keep one and leave behind the other. So I hold his love eternally with me, but lay the secret down for the living. I become afraid, sometimes, that it will be too late, that I will die before I see you again, hold you in my arms again, complete the story I've started to tell you. I become afraid that this story – your story – will never be told. It will be left unfinished, like the love that engendered it.

"Please let me come in, Sharifa, and I swear I will never trouble you again," Evan gently held the door frame as she opened it a crack. "I have to talk to you just one more time."

Sharifa lowered her eyes, opened the door and stepped aside to let him in. She closed the door behind them but stayed where she was.

He walked in, removing his hat and placing it on a chair near him, then he turned to her.

He breathed in deeply and when he spoke, his voice was ragged with emotion. "I can not undo the past, Sharifa, but what happened to you was my fault," she quietly protested but he raised his hand to stop her. "I know nothing I do can take away the violation," and he paused at the word and what it conjured and momentarily closed his eyes, "but I can try to make life a little easier for you from here onwards."

He fumbled in the pocket of his overcoat and pulled out a parcel wrapped in brown paper.

"I want you to have this," and he held it out to her, but his eyes were downcast. "It's not a lot, but you could put it towards the boys' education."

"I can not take that from you," Sharifa's voice was quiet but resolute.

"Why not? Oh, God, have I insulted you?" and Evan, suddenly looking exhausted, brought his one hand to his eyes and rubbed them hard.

"I know your intentions are good, but I can not take money from you," she repeated, looking down at the floor.

"Of course. Of course. Once again I've been foolish and naïve." He shoved the parcel back into the pocket of his overcoat and hung his head. "Sharifa, what am I to do? I just don't know what to do." And his voice began to break.

"Live your life, Evan. Be the good person you are. Help people learn how to read and write and make the world a better place." Sharifa had taken a step towards him and looked directly into his eyes. She was startled how much of Ali she saw in them, like the way the green flecks, dark with emotion, brightened when he smiled. Even when it wasn't his usual smile, but sad and slow.

"And you, Sharifa, what about you?"

"I have my sons, and I have my faith, and they will sustain me," she said, clasping her two small hands together in front of her.

'Then this is it?"

"I don't see any other way." She looked at the ground again.

"What will you tell your son when he's older, what will you tell..."

"Ali."

"What will you tell Ali?"

"For now I'll tell him, over and over again, how much he is loved. And thanks to you, perhaps one day I will tell him the rest in a letter."

He looked at her and his eyes were shining. "You've carried on learning?"

"You told me I could never give up," and the corner of her mouth tightened into a smile. "It is so hard that sometimes I really want to, but then your words come back to me. I am not good at it, and I doubt I ever will be, but you have given me the gift to write my sons' names and my own, and, most important of all, that of my creator. Allah."

"Sharifa…" and Evan sucked in his breath to try to calm his emotions.

She took a step towards him and took his hand, then covered it with her other. "Don't be sad. You have your whole life ahead of you."

"It doesn't feel like much of a life right now. I've walked away from everything and I'm not sure where to go next."

"It's a fresh page in a brand new book, use it to start a new story, a better one." She squeezed his hand once tightly and then let it go and took a step back. "It would be best now if you left, a neighbour could come by, or…"

"No, of course, I should go." He reached for his hat and fidgeted with it in his hands. "I don't know how to say good-bye."

"Then don't."

She raised her eyes and they looked at each other. He put his hat back on his head and tipped it lightly as he used to do all those times they walked together on the hill, then stepped around her and out of the door.

Only then did Sharifa allow herself to cry. And standing there, her back to the door and her small shoulders hunched, she wondered if she would ever stop.

CHAPTER FORTY-SIX

2015

NATALIE WANTED TO cry out, to scream, but her voice was locked in her throat. The man seemed at first completely oblivious of her and then, slowly, he raised his bloodshot eyes.

He made an indistinguishable sound and started to walk towards her, shrouded in the clouds coming out of his little pot. He stepped around the mound and Natalie took a step backwards, the spiney arms of a thorn tree poking her in the back and making her stumble forwards again.

"Who are you?" she called out, her arms outstretched as if to keep him at bay. "Where's my little girl? Where's Tamara?"

Afterwards, Natalie couldn't remember which she heard first, the wild thrashing in the bushes behind her or the inhuman roar. Later when she thought back to that moment, they were simultaneous.

Calvin burst out of the bushes and ran head-long towards the man, throwing him to ground and landing on top of him. He grabbed the man's dark collar with his left hand

and drew back his fist with the right, bringing it down with a crack on his face. He was drawing his fist back a second time when they heard the scream.

"No, Calvin! Calvin, stop! Please stop! He's my friend!"

Tamara ran into the clearing and straight towards Calvin.

It took him a moment to register, then he let go of the man and leapt to his feet. Tamara ran towards him and he bent down and threw his arms around her, hugging her tight and then lifting her off her feet to hug her a little tighter.

Natalie, at first too shaken and alarmed to move, ran towards them and Calvin gently put Tamara down and watched Natalie drop to her knees, weak with relief and exhaustion, and hold her daughter close, sobbing breathlessly into the little girl's hair.

Calvin put his hand out to the man who took it and allowed Calvin to help him up. But the minute he was on his feet he ran to retrieve his burning pot and retreated into the bush.

"Tamara, my love, what happened? We've been sick with worry," said Natalie when she finally loosened her grip on her and held her slightly away so she could get a good look at her. The little girl's hair was tousled and her clothes dirty, but she didn't seem in any way hurt.

"I didn't mean to run away, Mama. I just wanted to go for a little walk because I was standing with my hands over my ears but I could still hear Daddy shouting and I didn't like it."

"And where did you go?"

"I walked around the block and when I tried to come back I took the wrong road and got turned around. There were some naughty men by the bottle store and they were drunk and shouting at me and one started following me and I was scared.

"And then he," she pointed into the bushes, "he helped me. He came over to me and stood in front of me and waved his little pot at them. They were laughing but they also looked scared. They left me alone with the man and I tried to tell him where I lived but he didn't talk, he just walked with his little pot and I walked with him because I was lost and scared and didn't know how to get home."

Natalie pulled Tamara to her again, and held her very tightly. Calvin stood to one side but close enough to touch them, his chest still heaving with exertion and barely contained emotion that no amount of careful, controlled breathing seemed able to arrest.

They stood up, ready to leave and Tamara raised her arms to Calvin and he lifted her up.

"I can't leave without Polly," the little girl's voice was a tired whine.

"Where's Polly?"

"I dropped her and she got hurt, the man was fixing her with the muti in his pot." She pointed to the mound on the floor and Natalie walked over and bent down.

She picked up the doll and smiled to see a piece of twine wrapped around her broken arm and a tiny little wild flower sticking out of her long, black curls.

"She looks all better to me," Natalie smiled, holding the doll up towards her, and Tamara took it and cuddled it.

"I want to say goodbye to my friend," she whined again.

"Yes, we must say goodbye – and thank you – to him," Natalie looked across at Calvin.

He gently put Tamara down on the floor and she leant against her mother, resting her head on her hip.

Calvin walked towards the edge of the clearing and called out but there was no response. They could see the curls of black smoke rising and knew he was close by and most probably watching them.

Calvin reached into his pocket and took out some money and then laid it pointedly on the floor.

"Siyabonga, baba," he said softly, and then slowly backed away.

Then he walked back to Natalie and Tamara, lifted Tamara into his arms and with his hand on Natalie's back they made their way back to the car.

Tamara was fast asleep on her mother's lap when they reached their house and didn't stir, not even when Natalie gently wiped down her hands, face and feet with a warm face towel, changed her into her nightie and tucked her into bed. After calling Harry to tell him they'd found Tamara and all was well, Calvin made to leave.

"You don't have to go," Natalie looked at him.

"I have some unfinished business."

"Calvin, don't do anything rash, Tamara is home safe and sound, and that's all that matters."

"And that asshole is still hanging around the bottle store and fucking with people," said Calvin darkly. "He has to pay for what he did."

"Just be careful."

"Jah," he said and walked out the door. Natalie locked the door behind him and was turning to walk away when she heard a knock.

"Nat, open up, it's me." She unlocked and opened the door. "Can I borrow your wheels 'n go past the cop shop."

"Yes, yes of course. I'm glad you're not going to try and do this alone."

"Jah, after the treatment he gets from the po-po, he may wish he'd taken me on alone."

Natalie smiled and handed him the car keys.

"I'll bring back your wheels soon as I'm done."

"Sure."

He started back down the kitchen steps then stopped and turned around. "And then maybe, if it's lekker with you, I'll stay over."

"I'd like that."

She couldn't see his expression in the dark but imagined the corner of his mouth tightening into his characteristic lopsided smile.

She closed the door again and walked to Tamara's room. Then lay on top of the cover and put her arm around her little girl – and held her very close as she lay listening to her steady breathing.

CHAPTER FORTY-SEVEN

1924

THE LAST TIME Sharifa saw Evan, his son was almost the same age Ali would have been the day he came to the house to give her money. He was holding his little boy's hand and had a pile of books under his other arm. They met not far from the church where Sharifa had started her lessons. He looked every bit the school teacher, with chalk on his jacket and fingers stained black with ink. He didn't recognise her at first. She looked so much smaller than he remembered, and although her head scarf covered her hair, more grey than black these days, her once pitch-black eyebrows were streaked with white.

Time hadn't left him untouched either; he had snaking lines at the corners of his mouth and his once long, straw-coloured hair was thin and wispy, barely covering his suntanned scalp.

"Sharifa." She glanced up at him and he was smiling that familiar smile she had come to know so well. She was happy to see that his eyes, creased at the corners, danced with light, as they'd once done so long ago.

Then he went down on his haunches and whispered to his little boy, "Steven, this is one of my first students, she is a very special and very brave woman. Say hello."

Steven was staring at her head scarf.

"Hello," he said shyly. His eyes were dark brown and serious, and nothing like his father's.

Sharifa smiled and whispered, "Hello Steven."

Then Evan straightened up and although Sharifa didn't raise her eyes she could tell by his voice that he was smiling.

"We have a growing number of Moslem women joining our classes these days."

"Yes, I have heard. It has caused a bit of an uproar in the community," and she glanced up quickly and smiled. "But I tell them a bit of an uproar is sometimes a good thing."

He smiled back, with all his old ease and warmth, then taking Steven's hand again, said, "I am so happy to have seen you," and tipped his hat. They carried on walking in opposite directions, and Sharifa's heart suddenly felt too big for her chest.

CHAPTER FORTY-EIGHT

Sharifa 1954

In the end, my darling Ali, I waited too long to tell you. But how was I to know that Allah would call you home to Him so soon? There were times I grew angry with Him, when I raged at Him for taking you away from me. Times when I would pray, crying, and asking Him through my tears if taking you was punishment for my sins. But now that I have finally met Rudo and my beautiful Leila, I see that Allah gave you nothing but blessings in your short life. You knew love and you lived love, and can there be any greater gift than that? My heart breaks, my beloved son, to think I will never see you again on this earthly plane, but it is lifted when I think of our reunion one day in Jannah. I feel, dear Ali, that day drawing closer and closer. I have completed what I had to do and now I am ready. And although you will not hear it from my lips, perhaps when we meet in the after-life we can sit side-by-side, I can take your hand in mine and we can talk for hours on end. How my heart sings when I imagine that day, may it not be long now till Allah wills it.

The last few days I have not been able to leave my bed, but Rudo has come to my room for fajr just as we always did, and sat on the bed beside me holding my hand – and it was sitting like that, this very morning, that I finished telling her everything. I have felt her pain as I've told her our story, and it has pained me to see her cry. She has squeezed my hand many times, and turned to me in the early dawn light with so much love and understanding in her eyes I am moved to tears myself. She is now the custodian of our story here on earth, my darling Ali, as I knew you would have wanted her to be. And if she chooses to tell my sweet Leila, as she has promised she will, I hope she will remember to tell her that, above all, I loved you. With every single breath in my body. I loved you. And that love lives on through all those we leave behind.

I told you my story may not start where you may imagine it would. That it would start with me asking if you remember how the Namaqualand daisies bloom in July, setting the fields on fire; or how, on a clear September morning, Table Mountain seems to rise up from the ocean and tower over our beloved city like a benevolent giant. I would ask you if you remember what home feels like. That, I would tell you, is what love feels like too. And soon, my beloved son, I will be coming home to you.

CHAPTER FORTY-NINE

2016

"WHAT ARE YOU doing up so early?" Calvin was stretching as he walked over to Harry, kneeling by the flower bed in front of the veranda and digging up the earth. Sabrina, never far out of sight of her grandfather, was sitting in a wheelchair close by and Calvin walked over and kissed his niece on the crown of her warm head.

"Tal left early for work, she's got her first accounting exams coming, and Sabrina and I wanted to get these seeds into the ground before the rains come."

"What seeds?"

"Daisies. Namaqualand daisies from Cape Town, where my Nani Sharifa was from. I've been keeping them for a long time, from when Emma and Peter were children. I was keeping them for a special occasion, for an opportunity to celebrate new beginnings." He glanced up at Calvin and smiled.

Calvin smiled out of the corner of his mouth. "My o' man the romantic."

"There's more than a little of your o' man in you, son," and he slowly straightened one leg and then the other and stood up. He dusted his hands together and looked up at Calvin. "If my calculations are correct, these daisies are going to be blooming brighter than the sun by the time Natalie and Tamara move in and the baby comes."

"Ya scheme?" Calvin looked over at the bare flower bed.

"I scheme." And he smiled.

"Dad…"

"Yes son?" Harry looked up sharply at the seriousness of his tone.

"I don't wanna fuck this up."

The old man reached over and gently stoked Calvin's forearm and rested his hand there as he spoke. "I know, son. And I'm not going to say it will all miraculously be OK, I can't promise that, though I wish I could. But what I do know is that you've watched long enough how to do it the wrong way," and Harry sighed, "and you know how that hurt. Use the lessons you've learnt to do it the right way. It is frightening, no doubt about that. Love is just about the scariest thing you'll ever encounter."

"And ya scheme that's supposed to make me feel better?"

Harry smiled.

"I said just about the scariest thing. You know what the outright scariest thing is? To not love – and for all the pain it causes, I wouldn't wish that on my worst enemy. It's never all roses, you will make mistakes – everyone does – but what I ask is that you keep working at it, you keep trying. You have a real stab at a new start, hold on to it tight." And Harry's voice began to break.

Still holding onto Calvin's arm, he closed his eyes and steadied his emotions. Then, with a sharp intake of breath, he opened them again and looked up at Calvin.

"Right, enough of that. Now give me a hand with that hose pipe, son, I need to get some water on these babies, they've been waiting a long time to bloom."

CHAPTER FIFTY

"EMMA, HOWZIT!"

"Calvin, so great to hear from you! All OK with you guys? How's Sabrina, and Talia? Harry OK?"

"Jah, jah, everyone's lekker. I called to tune you some news. I'm having a lightie."

"You're having a what!"

"A lightie, a kid."

"Shit, Calvin, I think after all these years I should know what a lightie is! I just can't believe what I'm hearing! This is amazing news! Congratulations! Are you happy?"

"Jah, it's gonna sound mal, but I am."

"Why should that sound mal?"

"There's been a span of shit in this family, as you know, and I used to think lighties and shit – by the way, my chick – my girlfriend – Natalie already has a daughter, Tamara, so jah, I'm going from no lighties to two, can you fucking believe it – so, jah, I used to think lighties and shit would just make things even more complicated, be bringing more people into this world to have to live with the shit. But these last couple months I've been scheming maybe this is our chance to turn things around."

"You've paid your dues, Calvin, you deserve a little happiness – you all do. I just think this is the best news ever!"

"Ya scheme?"

"I scheme."

"I've spoken to Nat about you oeuns and she'd like to meet you."

"I'd love to meet her too. Hey, any woman brave enough to take you on is definitely worth meeting!"

"So when you coming back for a visit?"

"Well now that I know there's a little Calvin on the way, I'm going to start saving for a ticket today – coz I'd pay any amount of money to see you changing diapers!"

"Jah, jah, like hell! Listen, I've told Nat a lot about the o'queen too, and I've tuned her that if it's a girl I wanna call her Elizabeth. Wat ya scheme?"

"OK, now you've got me all teary," and Emma's voice started to break.

"Shit! Still with the waterworks – after all these years!"

"Yes, Calvin, still with the waterworks. I think that's such a beautiful idea, and if she has just a tenth of Elizabeth's beautiful nature, she'll be set for life."

"Jah, jah. And how about you? Any dudes on the horizon?"

"Hey, we're not going to dampen the mood with the sordid details of my dismal love life! For now I'm done with men and focusing on my studies."

"So how much longer till you're trying cases?"

"Why, you planning on needing a lawyer any time soon?"

"All I'm tuning is it's good to know there's gonna be one in the family – just in case."

Glossary

Aks – ask [slang]

Allah – God

Alhamdulillah – praise be to God

A span – a lot [slang]

Asr – Moslem mid-afternoon prayers

As Salaam Alaikum – peace be upon you (reply: Wa Alaikum Salaam – and may peace be upon you, too)

Bra – brother/dude [slang]

Cabin – home/house [slang]

China – friend [slang]

Cut – leave [slang]

Dhuhr – Moslem mid-day prayers

Du'a – prayer

Fajr – Moslem dawn prayers

Graft – work [slang]

Graze – food/eat [slang]

Gun 'em – beat them up [slang]

Hafizna Allah – may God protect us

Haraam – forbidden

Hijab – head covering

Huck – steal [slang]

In Shaa Allah – if God wills it

Jah/ja (silent 'j') – yes [slang]

Jahannam – hell

Jannah - paradise

Jinn – an evil spirit

Jol – go/come/party [slang]

Ka'bah – the most sacred site in Islam

Kafir – non-believer

Lekker/lakkar – nice/cool/good [slang]

Lightie – child/youngster [slang]

Madressa – school for Moslem studies

Maghrib – Moslem evening prayers

Makarad – Coloured person/person of mixed race [slang]

Mal – crazy [slang]

Ma Shaa Allah – God's will is being done

Masjid – Mosque

Mehndi – the painting of hands and feet with henna before a wedding

Menses – people [slang]

Nani – maternal grandmother

Nikkah – Moslem wedding ceremony

O' bali/o' man – father/husband [slang]

O' queen – mother/wife [slang]

Ouen – person/man [slang]

Praat – talk [slang]

Pump 'em – Beat them up [slang]

Scheme – think [slang]

Shalwar kameez – traditional dress comprising loose, lightweight trousers and long tunic tops

Sheets – money [slang]

Shukraan – thank you

Smaak – like/enjoy [slang]

Sut – no [slang]

Ta'zir – punishment for offences against the laws of Islam

Topi – Moslem skull cap

Tune/tjoon – tell [slang]

Wallah – I swear by God

Wheels – car [slang]

Ya – you [slang]

Yous – you, plural [slang]

ABOUT THE AUTHOR

VIOLETTE SOHAILI KEE-TUI was born in Bulawayo, Zimbabwe. She began her journalism career as an 18-year-old school leaver, training as an apprentice journalist on a local magazine before going on to work for a national newspaper as, initially, a junior reporter on the news desk. But she didn't last there long – her love for feature writing and her distaste for politics did not go unnoticed by her superiors and she was quickly transferred to the features desk where she rose to the position of Assistant Features Editor. During her time in the national media she won several awards, most notably Feature Writer of the Year in the National Journalism Awards. She returned to her studies after four years of working in the field, receiving an Honours Diploma from the London School of Journalism.

Driven by the need to tell the stories of people and communities, Violette became what some would call a narrative journalist – which should have been a natural progression to fiction writing. However, it wasn't until her mid-30s that she wrote and submitted her first short story – to the Intwasa Short Story Competition – for which she won third place. The next year she would take second prize in the same competition and, in 2012, first place, winning the highly coveted Yvonne Vera Award.

While a full-time working mom, Violette began writing her debut novel, *Mulberry Dreams*, in 2011, published by Pigeon Press in 2021. *Mulberry Dreams* was nominated for a Bulawayo Arts Award in 2022 and enjoyed both popular and critical acclaim. She was inspired to write *Magic and Masala* in June 2022, completing it at the end of the year. A mother of two, Emil and Katya, she still lives in her home town of Bulawayo. She and her partner, Paul Hubbard, own a gift and art shop in Bulawayo, and together run historical and cultural tours and activities in the city.

ALSO PUBLISHED BY
PIGEON PRESS

Fiction

John Eppel. 2019. *The Boy Who Loved Camping.* (Novella)

John Eppel. 2021. *Not the Whispering Wild.* (Poetry)

Violette Kee-Tui. 2021. *Mulberry Dreams.* (Novel)

Lewis Ndlovu. 2023. *Inganekwane: Parliament of Animals and Who's Wise.* (Children's Book)

Non-Fiction

John Eppel. 2023. *A Colonial Boy. Sketches of my life as a Rhodesian. 1950-1980.*

Paul Hubbard. 2018. *A Short History of Bulawayo. 1868-2017.*

Paul Hubbard. 2019. *Masiye Phambili! 125 years of Bulawayo's history: a timeline.*

Paul Hubbard. 2021. *Land of Strangers: A visitor's guide to Danag'ombe, Naletale, Zinjanja and Bhila Ruins, Insiza District, Zimbabwe.*

Paul Hubbard. 2021. *The Bulawayo Public Library: An quasquicentennial history.*

Terence Ranger, Paul Hubbard and Anthony Chennels. 2023. *A guide to the people and events associated with the "View of the World", Matobo Hills World Heritage Site, Zimbabwe.*

Collectibles

Bulawayo 2022 Calendar

Matopos 2023 Calendar

Bulawayo Postcards 2019

Milton Keynes UK
Ingram Content Group UK Ltd.
UKHW020749181223
434584UK00017B/1376